THE LAST KIDS ON EARTH

MAX BRALLIER & DOUGLAS HOLGATE

THE LAST KIDS ON EARTH

EGMONT

EGMONT

We bring stories to life

First published in the United States of America by Viking,
an imprint of Penguin Random House LLC, 2015

This edition published in 2015
By Egmont UK Limited
The Yellow Building, 1 Nicholas Road, London W11 4AN

Text copyright © 2015 Max Brallier
Illustrations copyright © 2015 Douglas Holgate

The moral rights of the author and illustrator have been asserted.

ISBN 978 1 4052 8163 8

www.egmont.co.uk

63721/009

A CIP catalogue record for this title is available from the British Library

Printed and bound in Great Britain by CPI Group

To Alyse, for support, advice, direction, and love and love and love. You're my cutie.

And another thing . . . This book is sort of a love letter to a group of great friends: Mikey, Mouth, Data and Chunk. Roberta, Teeny, Samantha and Chrissy. Angus and Troy. Gordy Lachance and Chris Chambers. Scotty Smalls and Benny the Jet. Corey, Haley and Jimmy. Thanks, friends – and thanks to all who made you.

– M.B.

To Allyson and Angus, may we never have to enact zombie plague survival plan alpha or beta, but know that if we do I wouldn't want to spend the apocalypse with anyone else.

– D.H.

chapter one

That's me.

Not the giant monster.

Beneath the giant monster. The kid on his back, with the splintered bat. The handsome kid, about to get eaten.

Forty-two days ago, I was regular Jack Sullivan: thirteen years old, living an uneventful life in the uninteresting town of Wakefield. I was totally **not** a hero, totally **not** a tough guy, totally **not** fighting giant monsters.

But look at me now. Battling a gargantuan beast on the roof of the local CVS pharmacy.

Life is crazy like that.

Right now, the *whole world* is crazy like that. Check the shattered windows. Check the wild vines crawling up the side of the building.

All of these things are not normal.

And me? I haven't been normal, well, ever.
I've always been *different*. See, I'm an orphan –
I bounced all over the country, different homes,
different families, before landing in this little
town of Wakefield in December.

But all that moving, it makes you tough:
it makes you cool, it makes you confident, it
makes you good with the girls – it makes you
JACK SULLIVAN.

Oh *crud!*

INCOMING MONSTER FIST!!!

3

KRUNCH!

CLOSE CALL!

Yikes.

Almost got a monster fist to the skull there.

I'm at CVS because I need an eyeglass repair kit – those little tool sets that dads buy for when their glasses break. I know, that's a lame thing to need. But I have a walkie and that walkie is busted and to fix that walkie, I need a really really *really* tiny screwdriver and the only place to get a really really *really* tiny screwdriver is in an **eyeglass repair kit**.

This was supposed to be a quick, easy trip to the pharmacy. But one thing I've learned about life after the Monster Apocalypse: **nothing's quick** and **nothing's easy**.

This monster here is the foulest, most ferocious and just plain horrible thing I've encountered yet. He's straight-up –

KA-SLAM!

Yikes! The monster's massive fist pounds the roof until it cracks like thin ice. I trip, tumble back and land hard on my bony butt.

It's time to stop being this monster's punching bag. See, I've kind of been the world's punching bag for a while and y'know – it just ain't a whole lotta fun.

So I'm fighting back.

I get to my feet.

I dust myself off.

I grip the bat in my hand. Not too tight, not too loose – just like they coach you in Little League baseball.

Only I'm not trying to hit some kid's lousy curveball . . . I'm trying to slay a monster.

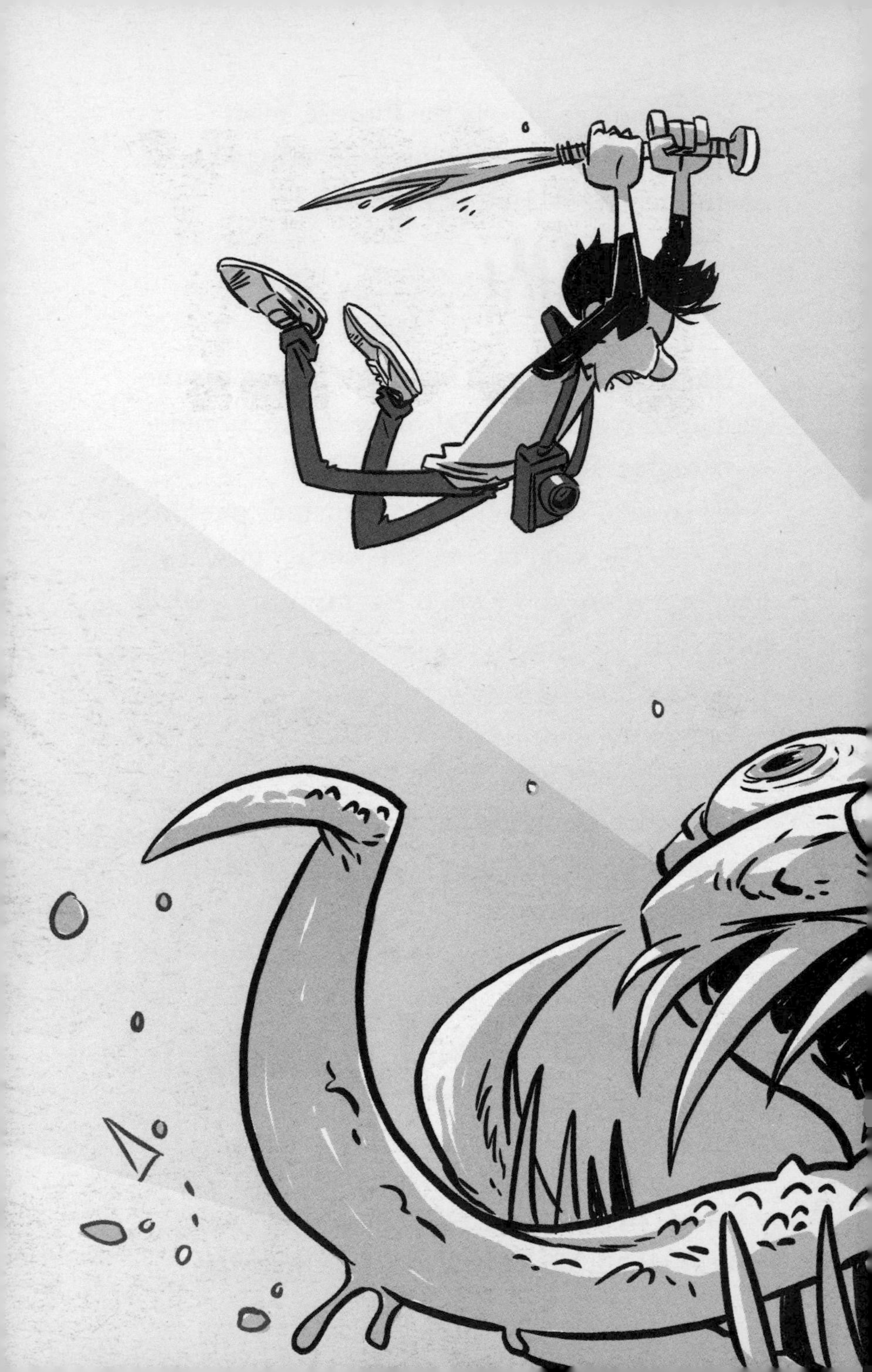

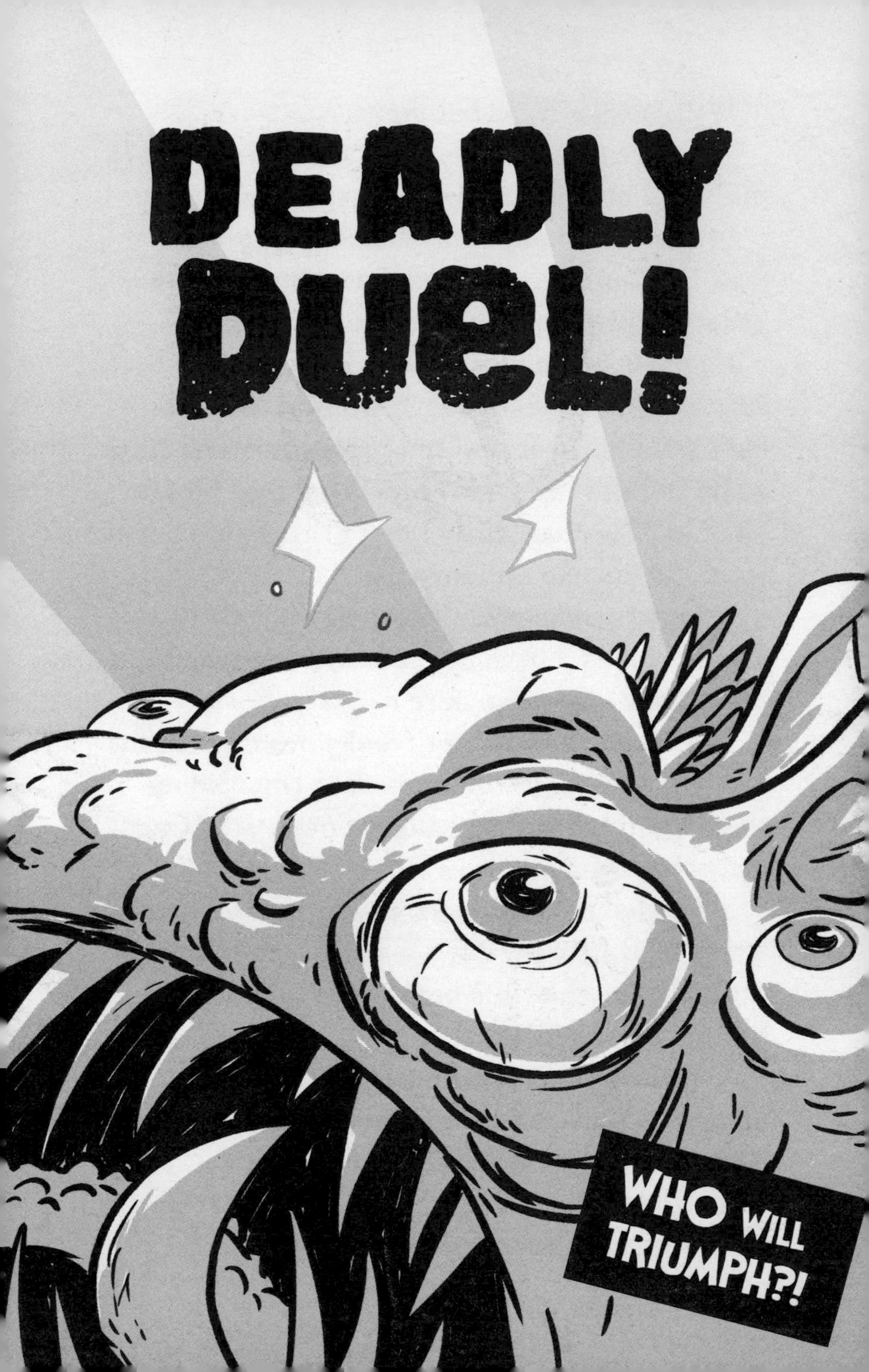
DEADLY DUEL!
WHO WILL TRIUMPH?!

Well, basically, *he* triumphs.

The monster's massive hand *snatches* me out of mid-air. I'm a thimble in his gargantuan grasp.

I try to grab hold of my baseball bat blade (aka the Louisville Slicer), but the monster's crushing grip pins my arms to my sides.

He pulls me in close to his face. Thick saliva, like slime, oozes down his lips. His eyes scan me over and his gaping nostrils flare as he inhales my scent. I feel like that blonde babe in *King Kong*. Only I don't think this beast wants to hug me and love me . . .

He sniffs some more, blowing my hair back as he exhales. I turn my face. His breath, it's just – **wow** – my man here needs to floss.

I've encountered other freaky beasts over the last forty-two days, but none like this. None that examined me: looking me over, smelling me, studying me.

None that felt this *terrifyingly smart*. I have a sick feeling in my gut – a sense – something that tells me that this beast here is 100% pure, beyond *beyond* EVIL.

A smile seems to creep across the monster's face. A sinister smirk that says, 'I'm not simply some primal thug. I'm a monstrous villain, a great evil, and I will enjoy inflicting pain upon your tiny human body.'

With a spine-tingling moan, the beast's mouth opens wide, revealing an army of dirty fangs, with chunks of flesh between each tooth. I kick. I squirm. And, facing imminent death-by-devouring, I at last BITE. My teeth sink into monster flesh and his paw loosens slightly – just enough for me to wrap my fingers around my blade's handle, rip it free, and –

I **slam** the bat into the creature's thick cranium until he roars – a sound like BLARG!!! – and his palm opens and –

Uh-oh . . .

I'm plummeting through the air, down through the hole in the roof, into the CVS . . .

I land in the junk-food aisle. I snatch an Oreo from its package and jam it into my mouth. *Mmm . . .* The Oreo is a whole lot stale, but whatever – an Oreo is an Oreo, and good snacks are hard to find these days. Plus, since the world ended, it's pretty much everything for the taking. And I'm not turning that down. No way.

Rising, I examine my predicament.

One of the monster's giant feet fills, like, the *entire store*. One toe in the school supplies aisle, another on top of the hairspray and deodorant aisle. Dashing up and over the monster's foot, toward the front of the store, I spot what I came for . . .

I shove the kit into my pocket. But then –

SMUNCH!!

The monster's clawed fingers tear through the roof like it's nothing. The ceiling collapses around me as I dart for the door. I'd love to stay for a while – flip through the magazines, check the sunglasses spinny thing for cool aviators, eat some cheese balls. But no time for that – y'know, giant monster and all.

I *burst* through the front door –

ESCAPE!

I dash past a crumpled car and through an overgrown yard, and slide beneath the caved-in porch of an abandoned house.

I pull out my camera. I *always* carry my camera. **Always.** I raise the viewfinder to my eyes, twist the lens, zoom in, and – **SNAP!!**

I photograph every monster I come across, so later on I can study their attacks and defences and strengths and weaknesses and junk. Also, it's just rad to say, 'I'm a monster photographer.'

I give each monster a name, too. But what to call this guy? What to call a monster so terrifying that just looking at him scrambles my insides with french-fried fear?

The big beast roars again, a sound like '**BLARG!**'

Hmm. *'Blarg.'* That's got a ring to it . . .

Suddenly, there's a racket like a wrecking ball crashing into ten million bits of Lego. The CVS is crumbling, collapsing, as Blarg stomps through its walls into the parking lot. When the smoke clears, I see the monster, fully, for the first time

– upright, standing tall on legs as thick as tree trunks, a monumental terror. He is . . .

BLARG

Blarg lowers his nose to the ground and sniffs. He lifts up a car and peeks underneath. Holy crud, he's on the hunt! He's searching! For me!

He scans the destroyed, decaying surroundings. He watches the porch. The porch I'm under . . .

I gulp. Can he see me?

I slowly inch backward, farther into the shadows.

He stares at the porch a moment longer, then raises his head to the sky. A deafening howl of frustration erupts from his lungs.

Guess he doesn't see me.

Blarg turns and stomps his way down Spring Street, away from the ruins of the CVS, sniffing along the ground as he goes. He's like a bloodhound, and now he has my scent . . .

As I sneak out from beneath the porch, I think, 'That was close.'

Super way dangerous close.

But I'm getting used to things being *super way dangerous close*. What can I say? Life after the Monster Apocalypse? It's scary. And also a lot *weird*. But that's OK. I'm a lot weird, too.

Now, time to get back to the tree house . . .

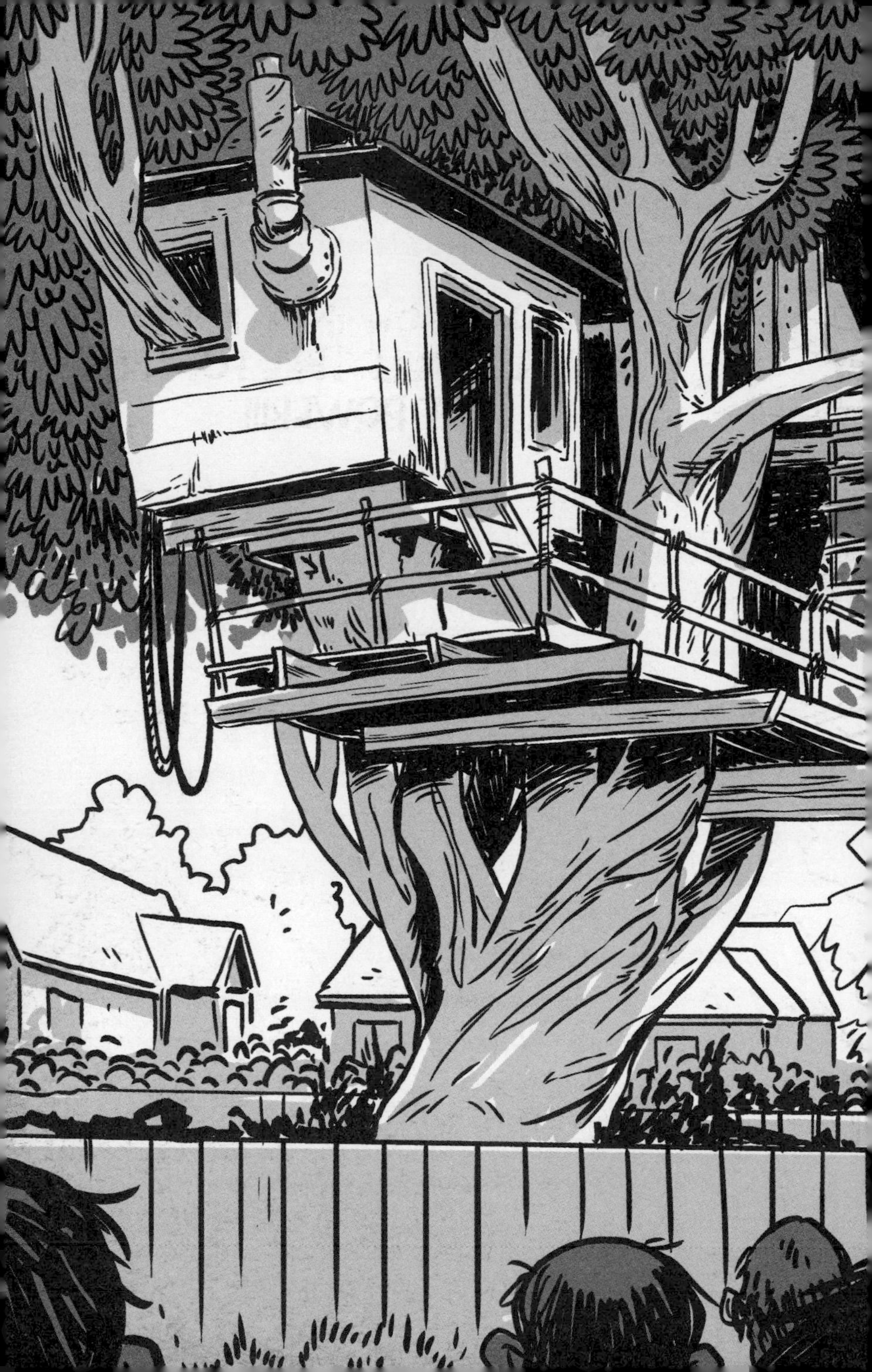

chapter two

JACK'S HIGH-IN-THE-SKY IMPENETRABLE TREE FORTRESS OF POWER!!!

This is where I live. I know it's not like a real-deal *home* with fancy junk like bathrooms and windows, but I think it's pretty OK.

The tree house *used* to belong to my scummy little foster brother. Y'know, before . . . But I've made some major additions since all the terror went down.

Now, why does a thirteen-year-old need a tree house that's better-defended than Fort Knox, Stark Tower, and the X-Mansion combined?

Because a MASS of zombie hordes and monster brutes have taken over Wakefield (and, as far as I know, the whole freaking world)!

You probably know what zombies are, but in case you've been living in a hole, let me break down the horror –

Classic Zombie

Those empty eyes – they're spooksville.

Constant, creepy moaning.

MMUHHH...

Bite you and you're one of them. Undead!

Stink like hot garbage.

Slow, until they get close – then fast!

There are other monsters, too.

Like the **Dozers** – big, hulking brutes that resemble two-legged rhinoceroses.

And the **Winged Wretches** – flying beasts like mutated pterodactyls.

And there are also the **Vine-Thingies** – long red vines that are alive. I mean, yeah, I know plants are alive – but these are like *alive* alive. They turn backyards into treacherous jungles!

Now, keep in mind, these aren't real-deal scientific names. I'm no monsterologist.

And all that's just scratching the surface. Almost every day I discover some new thing that is horrific and hair-raising and makes you wanna hurl.

Now, you're probably wondering why I'm telling you all this. Y'know, why you're privy to the thoughts and ramblings of a kid trying to stay alive during the Monster Apocalypse.

I'll tell you.

It's 'cause I think it's important that future people know what it was like in the time after the monsters arrived.

Also, I'd like to be remembered – just in case I get eaten one of these days. Like this . . .

Me, looking good while being eaten.

Now, *how* you remember me – well, only time will tell . . .

Zombie hunter?

Monster slayer?

Late-blooming, slow-developing 13-year-old?

Pick me!

21

Like I said, before the Monster Apocalypse I was an orphan. Well, I guess I still *am* an orphan, strictly speaking, but you know what I mean.

The last family I got stuck with – the Robinsons – they were the worst. As soon as the monsters showed up, they just hightailed it.

I wasn't all that surprised they left me behind. Honestly, I'm kinda sure the only reason they took me in in the first place was because they wanted someone to rake the leaves . . .

Now, if this sounds like I'm trying to make you feel bad for me or something – I'm not. That is *not* my style. I'm just letting you know the situation. The ins and outs. The deets.

I learned a long time ago that it's best to try not to worry so much about the junk life shovels on you. Life tries to knock you one – just do your best to duck and keep moving. The way I see it, *someone's* always got it worse, right?

I mean, unless you're the last person on Earth. Then, technically, yeah, no one has it worse.

Ever since the Robinsons peaced out – that's forty-two days ago, now – I've been forced to survive alone in a world of monsters. That's pretty much the plot of a video game, right?! So I said, y'know what, I'll *treat* life like a video game.

And that's easy, because I've always looked at life from a video-game-y angle *anyway* – picturing people's stats and powers and imagining obstacles like they're big boss fights.

You know how in video games there are challenges you complete to earn Trophies and Achievements?

Well, I created my own. I call them . . .

Feats of Apocalyptic Success!

I earn them by completing goals and challenges. The riskier the challenge, the greater the Feat. And I *always* need photographic proof. For example:

FEAT: Mad Hatter!
Steal the hats off five zombies.

FEAT: Outrun!
Beat a zombie in a footrace.

FEAT: Say Cheese!
Take a photo with someone you knew before they got zombified.

FEAT: House Hunter

Explore 50 different abandoned houses.

There are like 106 Feats still to be completed. And if I start running low, I just create more.

Now – pay attention – here's where things get serious.

There is one **VERY IMPORTANT** Feat of Apocalyptic Success that I have not yet completed. It is:

FEAT: Damsel in Distress

Find and rescue love interest, June Del Toro.

Here's *why* this particular Feat of Apocalyptic Success is the **ULTIMATE** Feat of Apocalyptic Success.

When I first moved to Wakefield, I decided I wanted to be a photojournalist (which is just a fancy word for taking photos of cool, action-y stuff).

When I told the Robinsons, they said, 'YEAH OK, *THAT*'LL HAPPEN!'

So I was like, whatever, I'll handle this on my own, and I got a gig taking photos for the school paper. That's where I met June Del Toro . . .

June Del Toro
- The Love Interest -

Hair smells like vanilla. And not that lousy American vanilla – French Vanilla.

Brain is smart. Total smart brain.

Legs that just won't quit (no idea what that means, I heard it in a movie. I guess her legs are resilient?).

She wears boys' sneakers. I don't know why I like that, but I do.

June was the student editor of the *Parker Middle School Gazette*, which was perfect, 'cause if we're both working on the paper, that gives us a reason to chat and get friendly, right?

Turns out, though, June is *scary* when she's on the job. But even when she's ticked-off and super-stressed, she manages to remain ridiculously cute . . .

Now, I should be clear here – I think June kind of **hates** me.

She told me I was lazy. I respectfully disagree. Not lazy – I was just trying to fulfill my role as *photographer*: the wild rebel who plays by his own rules, the hip cool guy who's always being hip and cool non-stop, 24/7, non-stop hip and cool, hip and cool.

June said my photos weren't capturing the important stories around the school. I guess she just wanted snapshots of bake sales or a pic of Ms Gradwohl's new whiteboard or something?

See, I don't go in for a lot of that boring junk. I like action! I like capturing that single moment in time that will never, ever be repeated.

And now? Now my camera is **full** of once-in-a-lifetime death-defying moments and crazy-close calls!

I mean, just this week . . .

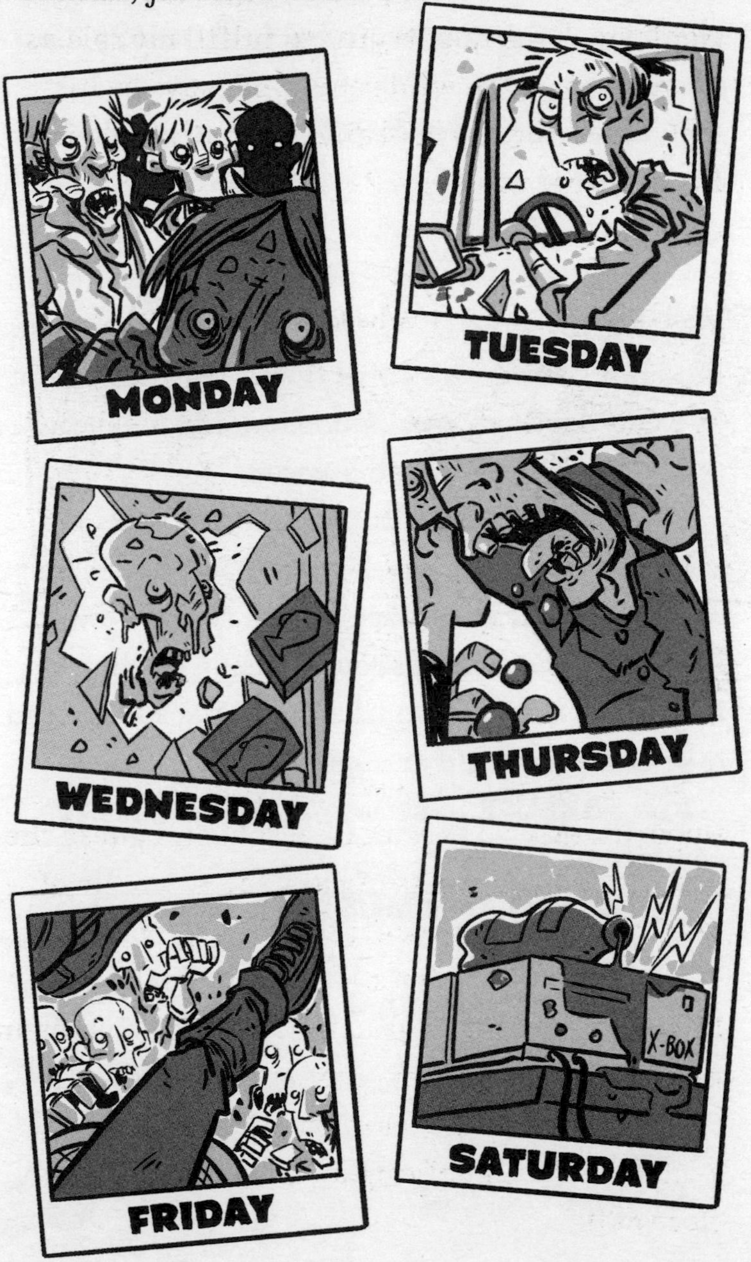
MONDAY
TUESDAY
WEDNESDAY
THURSDAY
FRIDAY
X-BOX
SATURDAY

Anyway, even though June maybe kind of hates me, I also maybe probably definitely kind of like her – a **lot**.

But is she still out there? Is she still alive? Is she still in town?

Here's what I know . . .

The day the Monster Apocalypse began I know **FOR A FACT** June was inside our middle school. But I don't think she's still there, because I went by a few days ago and I stood outside hollering 'June!' and there was no answer.

I'm also **VERY SURE** that June's parents *did not* leave town, because I went to her house last week and their cars were still in the driveway. I broke in and looked around inside the house, too, and it didn't seem like they'd packed up and taken off on a train or something.

And I **REFUSE** to believe that June has been zombified.

So that means she **MUST** be here, in town, somewhere.

So I'm going to find her. And I'm going to rescue her.

There you have it.

That's my life.

And that's my goal.

I will not rest until I'm done.

I'm a dorky warrior orphan. I'm a zombie-fighting, monster-slaying tornado of cool (not really, but this is my story, so deal). And I will –

Rescue June Del Toro and complete the ULTIMATE Feat of Apocalyptic Success!

chapter three

It's dusk and the sun is setting, all orange like a Popsicle. Rays of late-afternoon light shine through the tree house windows, and the little wind chime from HomeGoods I hung out front is dinging away.

I'm huddled over the busted walkie, trying to repair it with my new tiny little screwdriver.

Note! It's called a walkie. Not a walkie-talkie.

I think my repair job is going *pretty well.*

The walkie communicates with only one person: Quint Baker.

Quint Baker was – **IS** – my best friend! My *only* friend.

When I first moved to Wakefield last winter, Quint was the only kid who'd talk to me. When you're a foster kid and you bounce all around the place, you become used to getting by without friends.

But Quint and I were like Lego – we just clicked.

Quint gave me the walkie – one half of a pair – for my birthday. Best birthday present I ever got, ever. Since my foster parents were no way giving me a cell phone, and Quint's nutso parents were convinced cell phones made your brain melt, the walkies were the only way Quint and I could talk outside of school.

But now I'm afraid Quint is gone. The day everything happened, well . . . we split up. Now he's probably zombified or headed out west, along with everyone else in town. When everything first happened, I heard it was safer out west. But I haven't heard anything about that since, like, day four, so who knows.

But still, there's the chance Quint is alive, somewhere, and this walkie could reach him. So I cannot quit!

Seven finger burns later, I get the walkie working. I squeeze the button and it lets out a soft hiss that tells me it's transmitting.

Quint, it's Jack.

Finally got my walkie working. I have no idea if you're out there. But if you are, uh, well, let me know, buddy.

Getting a little lonely over here . . .

I wait a few minutes. No response. A few more minutes. Still no response. I head to bed.

My bed is a pile of sweatshirts and socks and towels in the corner of the tree house. I plop down and curl up under my one blanket. It's plenty warm out still, but I just need to be under a blanket when I sleep. I mean, a blanket isn't going to do anything against a Winged Wretch or a Dozer, but still – it just feels safer . . .

Soon I drift off to sleep. And I have nightmares.

Nightmares that feel *real*.

Nightmares about that morning, forty-two days ago, when *the monsters came and everything changed* . . .

42 DAYS AGO

It was a regular morning.

Early June.

After school, do you want to use sticks as lightsabers and sword-fight and film it so we can add special effects later and make our own movie?

Yes, Quint. Yes I do.

School was almost over and everyone had that summertime fever feeling – like freedom was just around the corner. I only half had it, because summer vacation for me meant a whole lot more time at home with the Robinsons, which was a recipe for zero fun-having and heavy lawn-mowing duty.

I remember, just before it happened, the bus pulling up in front of the school.

I remember, too, that Quint was eating this *rotten-smelling* egg salad sandwich. I can still smell it now – like the odour has been tattooed onto my nostrils.

And I remember Dirk Savage coming toward us. Filling the bus aisle. Thick and towering, casting a long shadow.

Dirk Savage was the most formidable bully at Parker Middle School. I think he came out of the womb with facial hair. Legend has it he moved here from Detroit and his parents just left him – they split because he kept bullying *them* – and he took up in a shack by himself way out in the Wakefield woods. He only showed up at school to steal lunch money from *other bullies*.

Dirk looked down at Quint and growled.

Kid, your sandwich stinks like squirrel butt.

Quint squinted up at Dirk. He didn't say anything. I mean, how do you respond to that?

Dirk snatched the sandwich from Quint's hand and jammed the thing – which he had just described as having the odour of squirrel butt – into his mouth.

'It stinks,' Dirk said, grinning a fat grin, crumbs tumbling from his big square face, 'but it don't taste too bad.'

I felt myself getting hot. Heart beating faster. Angry blood replacing regular blood, pumping through me.

I stood up. Tried to stay calm. Handle it cool.

I felt Quint's hand on my shirt, trying to stop me, saying 'Jack, it's fine . . .'

But it wasn't fine. I hate jerks – whether they're monster jerks or zombie jerks or just regular human jerks.

I shrugged. 'I'm sure we can find someone your size. Right, Quint?'

Quint looked out the window and closed his eyes and started humming to himself, like he wasn't involved in this. Sonofa . . .

I turned back to Dirk. 'Maybe a very rotund panda bear? That might be closer to your impressive figure.'

Dirk reached out and grabbed me by my collar.

'Hey, watch the jacket,' I said. 'It's a five-time hand-me-down. Might even be an antique.'

Dirk growled, 'You think you're funny?'

'I do. But to be fair, I also think people slipping on ice are funny. And guys getting hit in the groin. My sense of humour isn't exactly sophisticated.'

Dirk's about to slug me, when –

A high-pitched scream cuts through the air. There's always screaming in the morning outside school – people messing around, shoving, chasing, teasing, and girls laughing so loud it *sounds* like screaming.

But this scream was different.

It was a scream of pure horror. Dirk released me and I leaned over Quint and pressed my face to the window. And I saw –

ZOMBIES!

I remember thinking, 'UM . . . THIS CAN'T BE REAL. IT MUST BE A PRANK. A JOKE. A REALITY SHOW. RIGHT?!?'

So I said to Quint, **'UM . . . THIS CAN'T BE REAL. IT MUST BE A PRANK. A JOKE. A REALITY SHOW. RIGHT?!?'**

But it wasn't.

That was it.

The Monster Apocalypse had begun.

Next there was a Godzilla-sounding howl, like REARGHHHH!!!, and the whole bus suddenly shifted. I was thrown into Dirk, and Quint was lifted out of the seat and spun out into the aisle. The bus driver, a nice white-haired dude, was sobbing like a newborn.

The bus became darker. Something was covering the windows – wrapping around the bus.

A monster hand.

The monster tilted the bus so the back pointed toward the sky. We all pinballed, plummeting down the aisle, smashing against the seats, backpacks flying through the air.

We came to a sudden, painful stop, every kid on the bus piled up against the front door in a big heap.

'Quint?' I managed. I could barely breathe. Kids all over me. An armpit in my face. A foot on my head. An ear on my nose. 'Quint, what's happening?'

'I'm not sure, Jack,' Quint said. Quint always had the answer to everything. This time he didn't. That almost scared me more than the monster.

Almost.

This monster's hulking paw squeezed the bus like it was an empty Pringles can and the front door

opened with a loud metal **POP**, dumping us out onto
the parking lot pavement. My face bounced off the
cement. Nose bleeding. Blood trickling down onto
my lips and onto my tongue. I scrambled to my
feet, pulling Quint with me, leading us away from
the thick crowd and the screaming and the crying.

This is my nightmare now. That **was** a
nightmare then.

I got my bearings and looked around and –

TOTAL MONSTER ZOMBIE CHAOS!

One single, beautiful, angelic face stood out in the mass of fleeing people: June Del Toro.

I spotted a zombie stumbling toward her, coming up from behind.

'June!' I screamed, my voice cracking as I strained to shout across the parking lot. 'Behind you!'

June turned, dodged the stumbling, falling zombie, left it sprawled out on the ground, and darted inside the school. We locked eyes.

And then the door slammed shut.

I said to myself then that whatever happened, whatever came next, somehow I'd get back to the school and find June.

'Where to, Jack?!' Quint asked, snapping me out of it.

'Ah, Joe's Pizza? I think it's two-for-one slices today . . .'

'Jack, be serious!'

'Well, I don't know! Monster zombie chaos is new to me! I guess, ah, RUN!'

And we did. We sprinted away from the school bus and the giant monster and the hordes of zombies. We hopped the fence into the soccer field and fled to the woods beyond it.

'Quint,' I said, catching my breath and pulling him behind a tree. 'We need to find someplace to go. Like the police station or something. Or we need, like, G.I. Joe or the Avengers to show up. Or Iron Man! Something!'

'Iron Man isn't real, Jack.'

'The actor's real. I bet he could help.'

'JACK!'

'Sorry, you're right,' I said. 'He's probably busy being famous and stuff.'

Quint groaned. 'My parents are on vacation. I have a babysitter. I'll go to my house, assess the situation. You run to your house.'

I nodded.

Quint held up his walkie. 'We stay in touch on these at all times,' he said.

'Deal.' I was trying to stay calm, be classic cool Jack Sullivan, but my heart was pounding and it felt like my whole body was shaking.

When I got home, the car was gone and there were tyre marks in the driveway. My 'family' was gone.

I climbed up into the tree house. In my panic, I sort of collapsed onto the tree house poker table and knocked the walkie off. The walkie bounced on the floor and out through the door. I lunged for it, but –

I stared at the walkie on the ground below. I needed to talk to Quint, but – I'm embarrassed to admit – I was too scared to go down there. Too freaked out. Too overwhelmed. Too *everything*.

So I curled up on the floor. I pulled a jacket down over me. I put my earphones in to drown out the sounds of chaos outside.

And I stayed there. I stayed there for days, sleeping and waking and watching and waiting.

It got worse. Zombies everywhere. Giant monsters on the horizon. I blacked out the tree house windows and stayed put.

There was an old AM/FM radio in the tree house. For the first few days, newspeople tried to explain what was happening. I munched on Girl Scout cookies and potato chips while I listened to the radio guys say it was safer out west. But then, on the fifth day, there was no more radio . . .

So, I went back to sleep.

Just like I'm sleeping now.

When I finally worked up the courage to go out and do some exploring, it had been nine days since the madness in the school parking lot.

And in those nine days, *everything* had collapsed.

KRR-CHHHHHH!

A cracking, hissing sound wakes me from my flashback nightmare.

I blink twice. Not sure what's happening. Not sure where I am.

Again, *KRR-CHHHHHH!*

'What the huh?' I say, sitting up, rubbing at

my eyes. It's dawn. Sun is rising, blinding me.

Again, *KRR-CHHHHH!*

I slowly shake off the morning confusion.
I remember where I am. In the tree house. Forty-
three days after the Monster Apocalypse began.

And that sound – that *KRR-CHHHHH!* –
I realize –

It's the walkie!

I leap to my feet. Almost. One leg is asleep.
I fall, slam my knee into the floor, but shake it
off because I'm smooth like that. I half-sprint,
half-limp through the tree house, moving so fast
I bang my head on the doorway. I practically
dive for the walkie.

BZZZT!

Jack,
come in. Are
you there!?

Jack
here!

Jack on
the mic!

The voice on the other end of the walkie says, 'Jack, my friend. It's me. It's Quint.'

QUINT! He's alive!

But wait . . .

A horrible, terrible, *brain-poisoning* thought enters my mind.

Could it be a zombie trap?

Could the zombies and the monsters have started to *talk*? If they had, this would be the perfect ruse to lure me to my doom . . .

So I said, 'Ahh, Quint, buddy ol' pal. Quick question. You're alive, right? You're not, like, undead, trying to trick me or anything, are you?'

'I am very much alive, Jack.'

Phew!

Wait . . .

That's *exactly* what an undead Quint would say. Need to play this one cool.

'Quint, what's your favourite food?' I ask.

'Brains.'

'NOOOOO!!!!!'

But then the walkie buzzes again, and Quint says, 'Ha! Just kidding, friend. Brussels sprout surprise.'

PHEW!

I'm so relieved my best (only) friend is alive that I don't bust his chops about the fact that he's thirteen years old and his favourite food is Brussels sprout surprise.

'Dude, it's *really* you!' I exclaim.

'Indeed, it is. Shall we meet? I have much to show you.'

That's how Quint talks. He fancies himself a scientist, so apparently that means he needs to talk like an old geezer from the 1800s.

Don't ask.

'Yes!' I say. 'Hang-out time! Like before all this mess! What should we do? Video games? I have a generator, for electricity!'

'Yes, video games,' Quint says. 'We can play here. I'll see you in a short while, Jack.'

I smile. Ear to ear. Literally, the corner of my lip is touching my earlobe. 'Quint, that's the best sentence I've heard in my entire life.'

We 'over-and-out' and then I get to *really* waking up. Yawn, stretch, pee, touch my toes, hawk a loogie, splash water on my face from the bucket of rainwater I keep outside.

Time to plot a route to Quint's house – *and* add a new entry to my Feats of Apocalyptic Success.

In my Tree House Command Centre, I have a chalkboard I nabbed from the local elementary school after I finally remembered how brave I was and went out to explore. It's one of those giant ones that flip around so you can write on both sides.

It's super handy. Plus, I feel like an old World War II general every time I use it.

Last week, while exploring the library, I found an old map of the town from like the 1950s. I taped the map to the chalkboard and sketched my own little notes with important locations. As I learn more about the monsters and the general horrible things out there, I update it. Here's what I have so far . . .

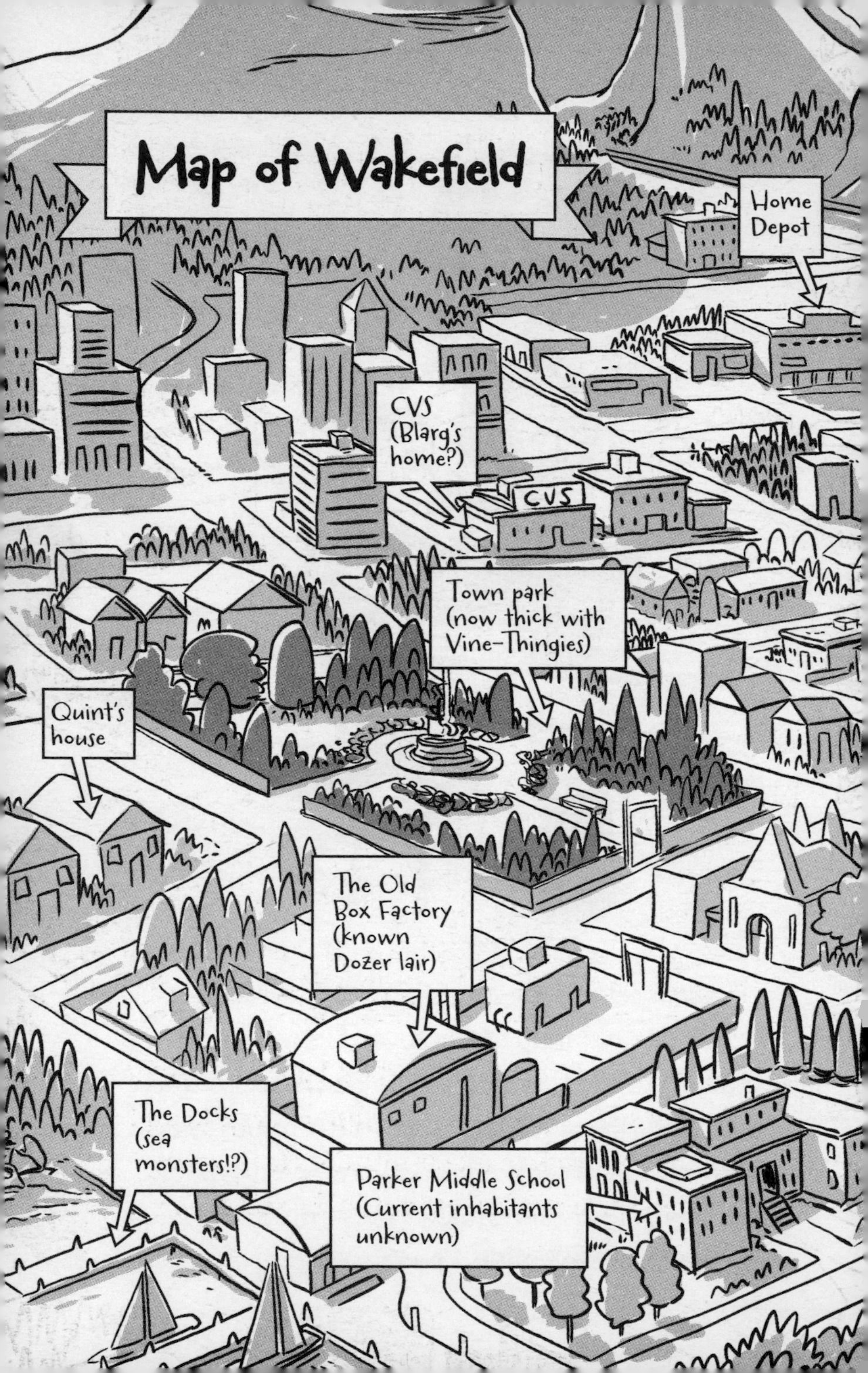
Map of Wakefield
Home Depot
CVS (Blarg's home?)
CVS
Town park (now thick with Vine-Thingies)
Quint's house
The Old Box Factory (known Dozer lair)
The Docks (sea monsters!?)
Parker Middle School (Current inhabitants unknown)

I plot a route to Quint's, then I suit up. Right now, my suit is pretty extra-super-terrible and lame. It's more like a last-minute Halloween costume than something actually useful for trying to survive.

The only *not-lame* part of the outfit is the weapons.

A monster slayer *needs* good weapons.

I mostly use this busted baseball bat – the one I got Blarg in the head with. I call it the Louisville Slicer, because it used to be a Louisville Slugger, but now it's splintered and sharp and it slices things and, well, you get it.

Louisville Slicer

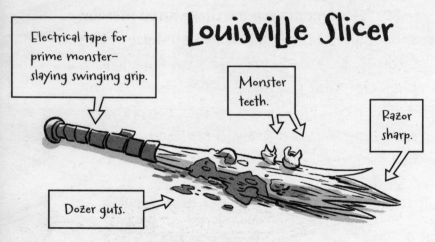

Electrical tape for prime monster-slaying swinging grip.

Monster teeth.

Razor sharp.

Dozer guts.

But I only use the Louisville Slicer on big monsters. *Not* on zombies.

See, I have a code, and the code says I don't cut up zombies.

The zombies *used* to be people! I mean, it's not their fault they're zombies now. I'm *not* stabbing these things that used to be people in the head with a splintered-sword-thing. Just not right.

So for zombie-fighting, I use a busted old hockey stick. Just a whack to the noggin and I keep moving.

I used to have a Wrist-Rocket (basically just a super-slick slingshot), but our science teacher Mr Mando took it on the third day of school.

Ugh, and my shoes . . . A really annoying thing happened with my shoes.

My foster mom gave me these hand-me-down shoes called Light-Upz. They had these little red lights that flashed every time you took a step. Basically, they're for pre-schoolers.

The first night I wore them out to play flashlight tag with Quint, I realized they weren't just dorktown – they were putting me at a tactical disadvantage.

One night after putting up the worst flashlight tag stats of my career, I got to work trying to slice out the lights, but that just made them sort of hang out of the shoe and look a whole brighter.

And then things got worse . . .

At school, stupid Nick DeRobertis told me that his cousin Silvio DeRobertis's ex-girlfriend's nephew's dogwalker stepped in a puddle wearing his Light-Upz and the water got into the lights and he got electrocuted and – **ZAP!** – he was fried right there on the spot. Not good.

So I wrapped the shoes in duct tape so you can't see the lights. They may be ugly, but at least they won't get me fried.

Anyway, Quint is like a super genius, so I'm hoping he can give my whole get-up – especially the shoes – a bit of a RoboCop-type upgrade.

Because right now, this is **me** – and I need some help.

JACK SULLIVAN

- The Hero -

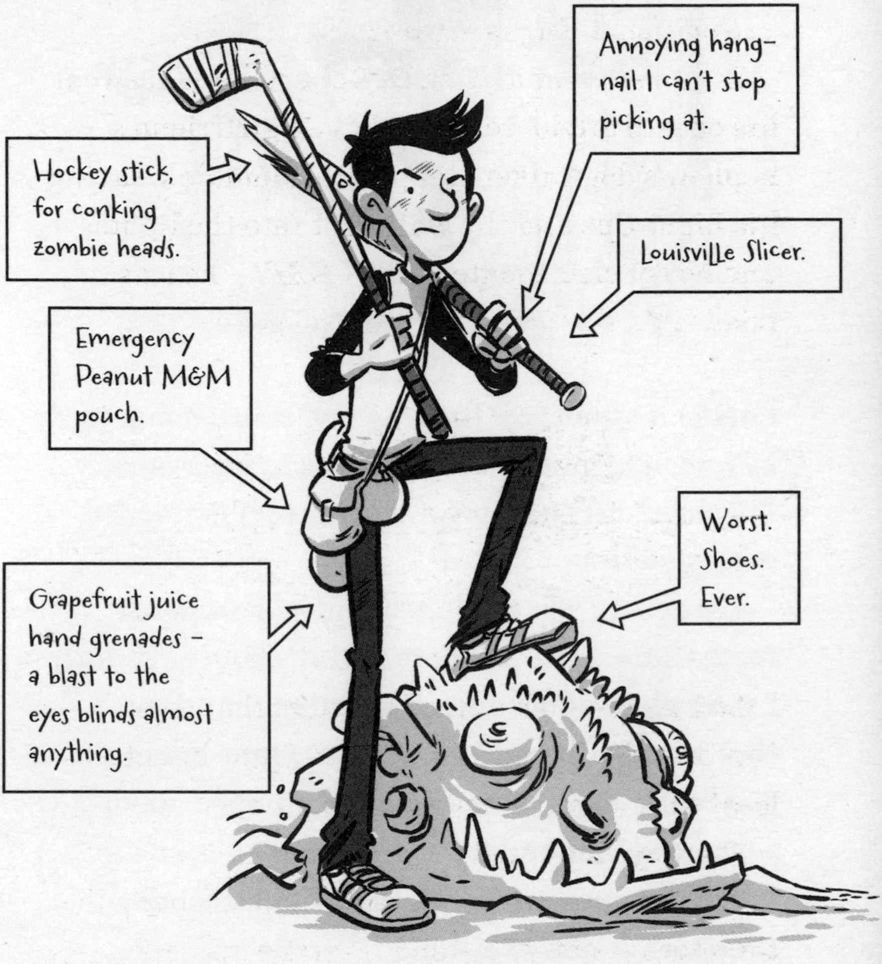
Annoying hang-nail I can't stop picking at.
Hockey stick, for conking zombie heads.
Louisville Slicer.
Emergency Peanut M&M pouch.
Worst. Shoes. Ever.
Grapefruit juice hand grenades - a blast to the eyes blinds almost anything.

chapter four

I make it almost all the way to Quint's house just by creeping quietly and sticking to backyards. But then I hit Oak Street. Oak Street is flooded with zombies.

I decide to hop the fence and go across the football field that borders Quint's house. Usually I steer clear of big open fields like that, 'cause they're a death trap, but it would take ages to go around and I'm just way too pumped about seeing my best buddy.

Halfway across the football field, though, I see I made a mistake.

Because halfway across the football field, I run into a Dozer. Dozers are just straight-up GIANT MONSTERS.

– Dozer –

Will eat zombies, but seem to prefer the living.

Travel alone, unlike the zombies.

Tusks for stabbing/ hurting/piercing/ other bad stuff.

Dead zombie. Oxymoron?

Super strong. Whip zombies around like rag dolls.

Thick skin protects internal organs.

Since Dozers were never people to begin with, I don't feel so bad when I destroy 'em. I just tell myself I'm being a monster-slayer.

'Cause I am. And that's awesome.

I reach for a grapefruit grenade – usually one of those to the eyes of a Dozer will stun it long enough for me to dash to safety.

But I stop when I hear a familiar, thundering roar – a second Dozer, behind me . . .

Double trouble!

I'm in a real pickle. And I hate pickles . . . I hate pickles the food and I hate 'pickles', like when you're in a jam. Although, funnily enough, I do love jam. Red raspberry, preferably.

Suddenly, out of nowhere, I hear a sound like *FLIIIITT –* **KA-SHMACK!**

WHUD!

It's Quint! My saviour! The only guy I know who would ever own a roof-mounted arrow launcher!

I sprint past the still-gurgling Dozer, leaving the second one in the dust. Down the dirt pathway, up and over the old wooden fence, and into Quint's backyard.

And there, waiting for me, is a whole *mess* of the undead suckers.

chapter five

The undead freaks come at me in a wave.

First, an old-man zombie – he's got one eyeball dangling out, and it bounces against his cheek. He lunges at me, his throat making a sound like **GLUGHH**.

I dive under his outstretched hands. Coming up, I'm staring at an old-lady zombie – must be like ninety. She gets my shirt but I shrug her off.

I can see the back door to Quint's house, and I spot a direct path –

The picnic table! I dash across.

KRAK!

I leap off the picnic table, using one zombie's bald, mouldy head as a little step, and grab on to the tyre swing.

Quint, open the door!

Quint yanks open the sliding door just as a hulking, half-rotten zombie man steps in front of it. His throat is missing – just a bunch of gnarly old flesh there. He comes at me, practically jumping. I've got no choice but –

KRAK!

Quint slams the patio door shut behind me. Just in time, too – three zombies stumble into the glass and bounce off like a bad slapstick routine.

Quint slides his big kitchen table against the glass – a makeshift barricade.

I get to my feet, eyes wide – I can't believe it. It's him. It's really him.

QUINT BAKER
- The Best Friend -

Hair smells like movie theatre popcorn butter.

Old-man cap.

Pocket watch for looking dorky.

Always working on a new gadget or experiment.

Wears a lab coat as a jacket. ALL! THE! TIME!

Non-athlete's foot.

'I was afraid you were dead this whole time!'
I exclaim.

'A scientist never truly dies,' Quint says.
'He lives on through his research.'

I groan.

'But yes, I'm also regular normal alive,'
Quint says.

I want to groan again, but I can't help but
laugh. I'm just so happy to see my buddy.

'Um, yeah. Remember?! We worked on it
that whole afternoon one time. We had that big
plan. We were gonna do the handshake when
we passed in the hallway so people would know
we had cool secrets going on and we were up to
stuff. Remember?'

Quint scratches his head. 'Vaguely remember.
How'd it go again?'

'Hmm. Um. You grab my ankle and I finger-flick your elbow. There was also some ear tugging, I think.'

Quint looks confused.

'Just tug my ear, Quint.'

'I am not tugging your ear.'

'C'mon. Just a little tug to get the handshake started.'

'Jack, I think you should give up on the secret handshake.'

I shrug. We bump fists. Can't go wrong with the classics.

I follow Quint up to his room: 'the lab',
as he calls it.

On the way upstairs, I pull out my list of Feats
and check off the box next to Make It to Quint's
House Without Dying. Another Feat down,
another pat on the back for ol' Jack.

Quint's house – the same house where I spent
almost every day after school for six months –
feels different now. But I can't quite wrap my
noggin around why . . .

'This is all research. I've learned much about our foes. It looks like we have three, possibly four creatures in the *Mammalia* class,' Quint says.

'Hold up, stop the train,' I say. 'I thought we were playing video games . . .'

Quint grins. 'A ploy.'

Sigh. I was right! It was a trap!

Quint continues, 'I'm about to begin classifying the monsters by genus and species, then grading their skill sets and abilities.'

'Grading their skill sets and abilities . . . You mean, like baseball players?' I ask.

Quint rolls his eyes. 'No, Jack, not like baseball players.'

'Like X-Men?' I ask.

Quint grins. 'A little.'

'Hey,' I say, suddenly realizing why his house seems so different. 'Where are your parents?'

Quint is silent for a moment. He stares at the floor, like he's studying it. 'They were on vacation, remember? So I don't know . . . I'm hoping they're out there, somewhere, maybe out west, safe . . .'

'Oh,' I say softly. 'And what about that weird babysitter they left you with?'

'Oh, she got zombified straight away.'

I laugh. Sort of. Half-laugh. No, less. One-third laugh.

After that, we just sit for a while – neither of us really speaking.

I cough into my hand and say, 'Hey, Quint. Is it true, what was on the news those first few days? That the monsters and zombies came to the East Coast first? So everyone went west, and out there the army was, like, prepared to stop them?'

Quint looks up at the ceiling. He thinks for a moment. 'I have no idea. I only know as much as I see. And what do I see? Monsters and zombies everywhere, very few survivors.

Internet down, phones down, no way to know anything else.'

'Do you think maybe *we* should try to go west?' I ask, even though I don't really want to leave.

Quint shakes his head. 'Absolutely not. Safest option is to stay here and stay safe. If help is going to come, we should be in a secure location, waiting for it.'

We sit in silence again for a while longer. Quint keeps his nose buried in his research while I half-heartedly flip through comic books.

The weight of all this horror – the missing parents, the zombified babysitter – fills the room.

I can barely breathe. I need to get Quint out of this house.

Finally, I stand up and say, trying to sound cheerful, 'Let's split, bud. We'll go back to the tree house. You have to see it! It's tricked out and way better than it used to be!'

But Quint, of course, is not having it. 'All my research is here. Can't leave. Not possible.'

'Buddy,' I say. 'I figured out how to make my own Mountain Dew.'

Quint looks up. He blinks twice. 'I'll gather my things.'

Quint says he has a 'means of transportation'
so I follow him down to the pitch-black garage.
It smells like gasoline and sawdust.

He flicks the light switch and what I see – man,
I have to pick my jaw up off the floor (not literally –
that is something zombies do). I'm staring at a
bad-to-the-bone post-apocalyptic vehicle!

'I began with my mom's pickup truck,' Quint says, 'and I just started adding things . . .'

I whistle, impressed.

'Now pay attention, Jack,' he says, and he begins detailing the truck's gizmos and gadgets. It's amazing what a smart kid can do when no one's bugging him to finish his homework or change his socks.

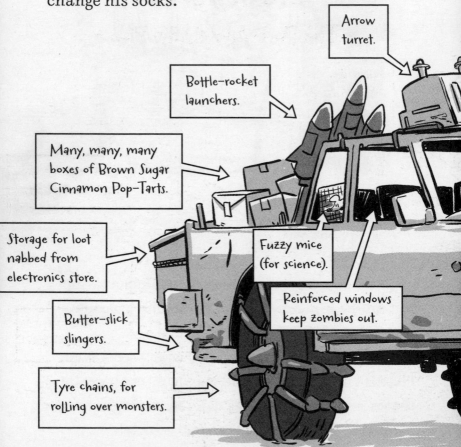

Arrow turret.

Bottle-rocket launchers.

Many, many, many boxes of Brown Sugar Cinnamon Pop-Tarts.

Storage for loot nabbed from electronics store.

Fuzzy mice (for science).

Butter-slick slingers.

Reinforced windows keep zombies out.

Tyre chains, for rolling over monsters.

Running my hands over the truck, I ask, 'So what do you call it?'

'Big Mama,' Quint says. 'After, well, my big mama.'

I nod. It's true. His mom was quite hefty. 'Perfect name, buddy.'

BIG MAMA
– The Post-Apocalyptic Ride –

Fuzzy dice (for looking cool).

Skull hood ornament (not real, just a candle).

Horn plays the *Star Trek* theme.

Battering ram, for battering monsters.

Plus, an ejector seat.

(just kidding)

We spend the next hour stuffing all of Quint's research and equipment and action figures into Big Mama. Once we have it all loaded up, Quint pauses. 'Um, one thing. Do you have any idea how to drive?'

'Dude, we're thirteen years old,' I say.

Quint's face sags. 'Right –'

'So I've played like two hundred hours of *Need for Speed*! Of COURSE I know how to drive. I'm practically an expert.'

'Jack . . .'

KA-SMASH!

We get back to the tree house with no major issues. Only roadblock is a zombie horde outside the old skating rink that forces me back toward the centre of town – past the ruins of the CVS.

Passing the store's remains, I slow down just long enough to see if Blarg is still hanging around.

I don't see him.

That worries me. Blarg is out there, somewhere, and he has my scent . . .

But I push the thought to the back of my mind. Today is a good day, and I'm not ruining it with thoughts of ginormous beasts.

And tonight is even better . . .

Quint and I are roasting marshmallows and getting ready to play some *Mario Kart*.

For the first time in a long while, everything feels right.

Quint has been found!

And now I'll use his mega-smart science brain to help me find June Del Toro and complete the ULTIMATE Feat of Apocalyptic Success!

chapter six

I figure there are two types of people in this world:

The first: People who think living in an abandoned, post-apocalyptic world would be awesome.

Anarchy rules!

Normal folks.

The second: Normal folks who think that people in the first group are clinically insane.

Quint is definitely type numero uno. Every day since he came to live here he's been up at the crack of dawn, 'doing research'. He says we need to document the end of the world properly, like scientists.

See?
This is what
I deal with.

On the plus side, Quint is a big fan of my photos – 'For science,' he says. I don't think he quite gets the art of it – he just says they're really helping with the whole 'studying the monsters' process.

Me, I'm less into 'studying the monsters' and more into, y'know . . .

> DESTROYING THE HORRIBLE MONSTERS THAT HAVE TAKEN OVER THE WORLD!!!

But whatever.

Different strokes for different dorks.

The problem is that all this research keeps reminding me that IT'S BUTT-CLENCHINGLY SCARY OUT THERE!

And when something is butt-clenchingly scary, it's natural to want to avoid it.

Maybe that's why I haven't gone back out to look for June in two days.

So tomorrow, I'm changing that.

Tomorrow, I'm going to be all Liam Neeson-y, like, 'WHAT'S UP, ZOMBIES?! HAND OVER MY FRIEND JUNE!'

Tomorrow, bright and early, we're scouring this town for June. Not just the school and not just her home. Everywhere. No building unexplored. No spot unsearched.

It's 6:45 in the morning and I'm guzzling a warm Cherry Pepsi, trying to put a little pep in my system. I give Quint a gentle kick to the side. He groans, groggy, looks up and mutters, 'Santa?'

'Quint,' I say, 'I need to complete my ULTIMATE Feat of Apocalyptic Success: find and, if necessary (which it totally will be), rescue June Del Toro.'

Quint grunts, climbs out of his sleeping bag, and shuffles over to our little bathroom. The bathroom is just a bucket on the side of the tree house. We have a rule – no one looks at what the other person is doing. You wouldn't think that would *need* to be a rule, but, well, Quint is odd, and stuff like this kept happening –

So whatcha thinkin'. Hot dogs for dinner?

DUDE!!!

Quint has another weird habit: he always talks while he's out there on the bathroom bucket. Today he says, 'Before we go driving anywhere, we need gasoline.'

See, we've been using gasoline by the gallonful to run the generator for the Xbox and the toaster oven and the RC helicopter and the massage chair and the Christmas lights and all that jazz.

I had what I THOUGHT was a brilliant plan to get us some easy electricity. Y'know those wheels that mice run on in labs and junk? Well, I was going to grab a treadmill from the high school gym and . . .

ZOMBIE POWER!

Quint said that idea was, and I quote, 'so dumb, Jack, that I'm not sure how anyone who would propose such an idea even manages to get dressed in the morning.'

I said, 'Whatever,' and pointed out that his pants were on backwards.

Anyway, I agree to get the gasoline – no choice, only way to find June. I suit up, down another Cherry Pepsi, and embark on OPERATION: JACK GETS GAS. Note – maybe need a new name for this op . . .

We've drained every nearby car, so I'm forced to venture farther . . .

APOCALYPTIC MORNING STROLL!

Look, I've missed out on a lot of things in life: big birthday bashes, trips to Disney, inside jokes, being part of a 'clique' at school – I didn't get that stuff, I know that – but for the most part, it's all good.

You know why it's all good?

It's all good because there's a feeling you get, when you're walking through a post-apocalyptic wasteland, and your weapon rests on your shoulder the way a longsword might have rested on the armoured shoulder of King Arthur – and man, it is a freaking killer feeling.

And that feeling, that freedom, that total independence – I don't know if I'd trade it for a thousand trips to Disney World or Disneyland or Disney Town or Yankee Stadium or Big Earl's Petting Zoo or wherever it is parents take kids. I mean –

'BLARGGGGHHH!'

The sound stops me dead in my tracks. The monster Blarg. And he's *close*.

I tiptoe to the nearest house and peer around the side, past a bunch of overgrown bushes.

'BLARGGGGHHH!'

That roar sounded closer.

A trellis runs up the side of the house, covered in wild plant life. Slowly, I climb up to the roof for a better view.

I spot Blarg's thick, armoured hide, tentacle-covered back and bug-eyed face rising above a big house, a few blocks south.

I watch as Blarg bends down, disappears behind the house for a moment, then comes back up, holding a zombie. He stares at it.

I gulp.

Could it be?

Does Blarg think that zombie is *me*?

Finally, Blarg's face gets tight, like he's ticked off. He roars and shoves the undead thing into his mouth. As he chews, the sound of the poor zombie's snapping bones echoes across the empty suburban streets.

My blood runs cold. I can barely breathe. I can't even think of something sarcastic to say.

I put my head down and I lie on the roof. I wait a long, long time before I move again.

———

It's nearly noon when I'm finally sure Blarg is gone and I climb back down the trellis. Now –

Find the gas. No delays. And hopefully, no Blarg.

Seven blocks from the tree house, I spot a minivan. Perfect.

The gas cap needs to be popped from the inside. I try the door. Locked. I step away, cock back the Louisville Slicer and – *KRAK!* – shatter the window. I pop the lock.

Inside the car, something catches my eye.

A sun-bleached photo, on the dashboard.

They look like the happiest family on earth.

And now? Now they're probably stumbling around Wakefield, bodies decaying and limbs falling off.

I can't help but think how they at least got to be a family. With a dog, even. At least they got to have a house – a real house, not some random place you just get shipped to every year.

A home.

They had what I've always wanted. Now they're zombies – but at least, for a while, they had it.

I was wrong.

I lied, before. It's not all good. There are a lot of things in my life that I've missed out on, but they don't have much to do with Disney.

I slam the door shut. Enough thinking about family and home. Don't worry, I'm not going all soft on you – I'm still mister jokey monster-blaster. Just sometimes – y'know – emotions, man.

I pull out a big empty Gatorade jug, unscrew the truck's gas cap, stick the jug beneath it, and the gas begins to flow.

That's when I hear the noise: a sort of soft growling.

I pull the Louisville Slicer from its sheath as I slowly turn.

Not sure what type of monster this is – I've never seen one like this before. It doesn't stink like death, which is nice.

The monster growls again, with more intensity.

I take a slow step back, and then –

The monster charges!

OH CRUD OH CRUD OH CRUD!

I turn to run and – **POW!** – slam into the side of the van. I hit the ground and the next thing I know, the monster is leaping, pinning me.

This is it. This is the end. I couldn't even last TWO MONTHS after the Monster Apocalypse! Some hero you are, Jack!

The monster opens its mouth wide and –

'Hey, monster, get off! You got dog breath!' I say, laughing, as I manage to get myself out from underneath the thing. Then it just sits there, big yellow tongue hanging out of its mouth, panting.

'Thanks for not eating me, pal,' I say as I stuff the Gatorade bottle into my backpack. 'Much appreciated.'

I give the monster one final look, then I begin the careful trek home. But the big ball of fur follows me . . .

After two blocks, I stop and turn and yell, 'Hey, you gotta beat it! You're a monster! I'm a, y'know, non-monster. You can't follow me!'

But it doesn't work.

Nothing.

I try speaking to him in monster.

Murgleblargleburghh!!!!

Still nothing.

'Look, it's like Romeo and Juliet, monster
dude. We come from two different worlds. It'll
never work!'

Ten minutes later, when I get back to the tree
house, he's still nipping at my heels. I push
through the bushes, and –

'HALT RIGHT THERE!'

That's Quint. Captain Observant. 'Buddy, I know. He followed me home.'

'Well, tell him to leave!' Quint says.

'I tried that. He doesn't understand English or my flawless monster-speak.'

'How do you suggest we proceed?' Quint asks.

'Well, don't shoot me, but . . . he *is* friendly. I say we let him hang. We'll have him in for dinner. You think he likes Pringles?'

'Jack, are you insane?!? Absolutely not! I'd love to study him and learn more – but it's too risky!'

'Quint, I hear you telling me no. But I think, I'm pretty sure, your eyes are telling me yes.'

'JACK!'

But look how cute he is!

Quint glares and huffs and grumbles, but after a minute, he goes back inside the tree house.

Guess that means he's cool with it.

And I guess that means I now have a pet monster. I think I'll name him . . . Rover.

I pull my list from my pocket and make a big, happy checkmark next to –

FEAT: Get an Awesome Pet

chapter seven

OK, this is it, no playing, no waiting, no putting it off because of something dinky like 'being horribly terrified'. We're scouring Wakefield for June. Quint says I'm nuts. Quint says it's a long shot. Quint says the odds of one random girl being alive in this town that seems to have *very* few survivors is infinitely small.

But like I tell him, that doesn't explain the feeling in my gut. He tells me the feeling in my gut is probably just gas and I sock him on the arm.

I say, getting all serious, that none of his reasoning can explain the look in June's eyes when I saw her go back into the school that day. A look that told me I'd see her again. And not as a zombie. I'd see her alive. And there might even be a hug involved.

So we're on the hunt. I'm behind the wheel of Big Mama, cruising down South Street, swerving back and forth across the road to avoid zombies and overturned streetlights and other apocalyptic litter.

First stop, Parker Middle School. I've been

there five times so far, standing outside, yelling for June. But maybe she just didn't hear me. So today, I climb in the truck bed, grab a megaphone I nabbed from the fire station, and bust out a new strategy . . .

June Del Toro! Are you in there? This is Jack Sullivan, Post-Apocalyptic Action Hero, here to rescue you.

Quint stares up at me from the passenger seat. 'Post-Apocalyptic Action Hero?! That's what you're calling yourself?'

I shrug. 'What? It's accurate.'

Quint rolls his eyes.

'Well, it's better than Jack Sullivan, Cheese-Ball-Loving Kid in a Tree House!'

'Well, then, I want a cool title, too,' Quint says. 'Quint Baker, Scientific Analyst.'

'You have the chance to give yourself any title you want and you land on Scientific Analyst?'

Quint shrugs. 'Scientific analysis is *cool*, Jack.'

I shake my head and go back to hollering at the school. We try for another ten minutes.

Nothing.

'Let's try the mall,' I say, slipping back into the seat and putting the truck in gear. 'Girls like the mall, right? That's a thing.'

But as I steer Big Mama up and over the kerb and through a mailbox, Quint suddenly screams, 'THAT'S IT!!!'

'Huh? What? Where?! What's it!?'

'I CAN'T TAKE IT ANY MORE, FRIEND!' Quint exclaims. 'You need to learn how to drive.'

'What are you talking about. I'm a killer driver!'

EVIDENCE OF KILLER DRIVING

Look, I think I'm doing pretty good for a guy whose total driving experience, up to this point, has been limited to holding an Xbox One controller and just squeezing the R trigger as hard as I could. But Quint doesn't think that's good enough.

Two hours later, he's got me down by the docks, driving through cones and practising three-point turns. Even the zombies are bored.

And then Quint starts in on the parallel parking . . .

Finally I say, 'ENOUGH! It's time we have a little fun.'

I gun it across the parking area. The engine roars. Big Mama is rumbling and shaking and the wheel feels gigantic in my hands.

'Incoming loading dock!' Quint shrieks.

I cut the wheel hard right and Big Mama swerves. We're careening around a corner, when – out of nowhere! – there is something **alive** in front of us! Whatever it is dives out of the way a moment before I hit it!

I slam the brakes and the tyres squeal as we spin to a stop. 'I think that was a person,' I say. My voice cracks. 'We need to get out and look.'

'Not necessary,' Quint says, watching the side mirror. 'It is a person. Sort of.'

Quint turns to me. His face is tight, like now he's the one having digestive problems. 'It's Dirk Savage.'

I look in the rear-view mirror.

Quint's right. Slightly shaking, I reach for the door handle.

'What are you doing?' Quint asks.

'He's a survivor. Like us. We can't leave him.'

'But I hate Dirk! He's the worst! He terrorized me!' Quint exclaims. 'I don't want him in our home. That's where I do my research, Jack. MY RESEARCH! It's my special place.'

'We can't leave him, Quint,' I repeat.

I can see the wheels turning in Quint's head. After a long moment, he says, 'Fine. But ask him to be nice to me!'

A horde of zombies have caught wind of us and are shuffling their way over. Need to be quick.

I step out of the car, and there he stands . . .

– DIRK SAVAGE –

Dirk towers alone in the middle of the lot, like some Wild West gunslinger. If there were tumbleweeds in Wakefield, one would probably roll past us just about now.

'Howdy, pardner,' I say, in my toughest tough-guy drawl.

Hello.

So . . . what do I say here? What are the rules now? How do we behave now that the world has gone down the toilet?

Suddenly – Dirk's eyes dart to the side. Uh-oh, was this some sort of trap? Are we being hoodwinked? Winked by hoods?!

No . . .

Worse . . .

'FLYING MONSTER!' Dirk shouts.

A bloodcurdling shriek from above, and then a grotesque beast is swooping down. It is a . . .

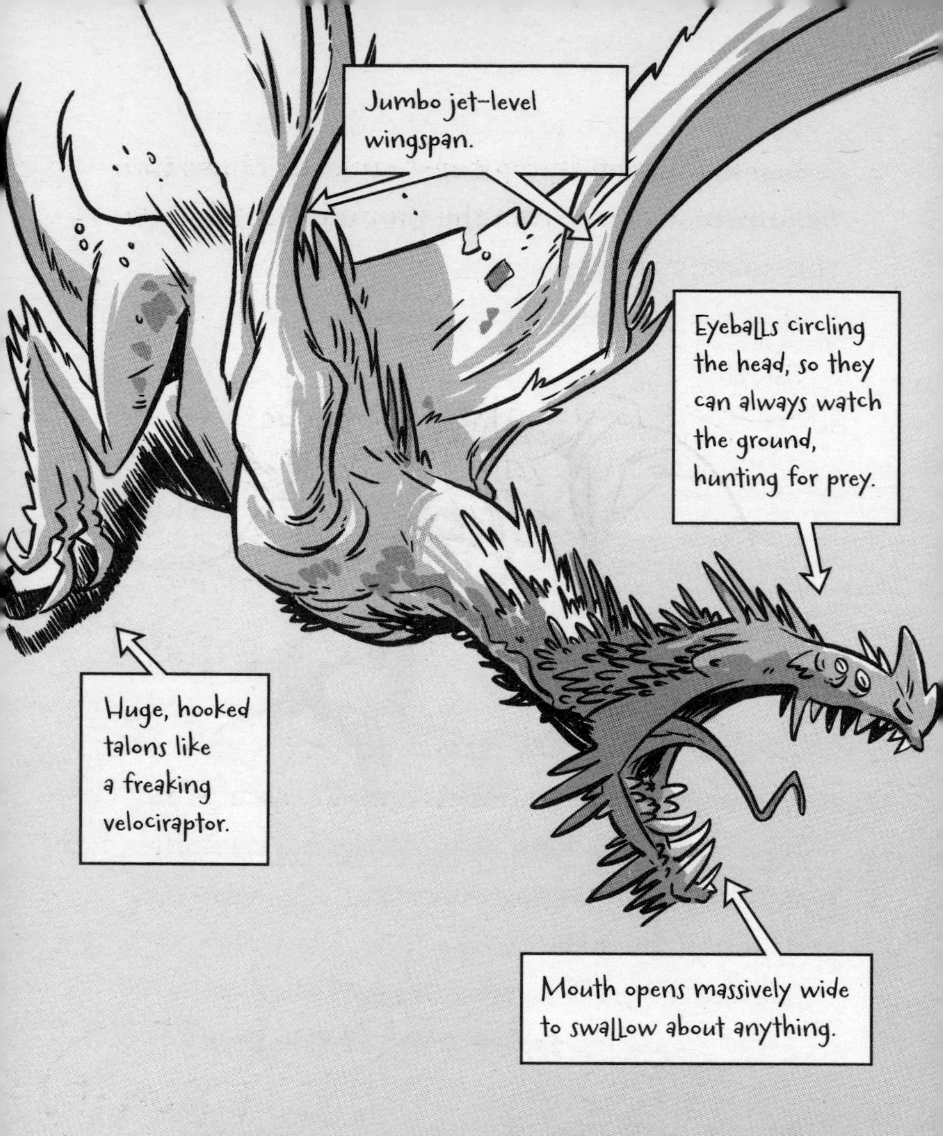
Jumbo jet-level wingspan.
Eyeballs circling the head, so they can always watch the ground, hunting for prey.
Huge, hooked talons like a freaking velociraptor.
Mouth opens massively wide to swallow about anything.

- WINGED WRETCH -

Just before the flying beast sinks its claws into me and plucks me from the ground, Dirk Savage shoves me aside!

The Winged Wretch circles around.

Dirk eyes the monster. His hands open wide. On the tips of his toes. Dirk is like a wild lion, all coiled up, ready to pounce.

And then he does –

MONSTER LAUNCH!

Whoa. I thought *I* was good at crushing monsters. Dirk is like Conan the Barbarian!

Dirk hurls the Winged Wretch into the closest building. Chunks of brick rain down. The monster lets out a pained howl, then flies off into the distance, sort of air-limping. We're safe.

Dirk gives me a short, hard nod – a super-manly 'You're welcome' – and turns to leave.

'Wait!' I call after him. 'Ah . . . Where are you going?'

'The monsters will be back. More of them. Need to get to cover,' he says.

I realize then that the bully/bullied relationship has seriously shifted. Dirk's clothes are torn and tattered. He is clearly alone. Dirk Savage needs my friendship more than I ever needed his.

'Well, um – do you wanna, like . . . hang out?' I ask. 'I'm with Quint, we have a tree house. There's room – I mean, if you wanted to . . .'

Dirk looks at me like I just asked him to slow dance. 'What would I want with you two losers?'

I don't respond.

After a moment, Dirk's eyes drop to the pavement. He kicks at an old cola bottle cap.

'C'mon,' I say. 'You can still do the whole tough-guy-loner thing. You just do it with us.'

Dirk says, 'Uh-uh. Can't be a loner unless you're alone.'

I sigh. 'Dude, I'm not gonna beg.'

Dirk looks up, then mumbles something that sounds like, 'Well, if it'll shut you up . . .'

Quint looks like he's going to toss his lunch when he sees Dirk climbing into the back seat. He begins rambling, 'Oh, um, hi, Dirk! Mr Savage – er, Mr Dirk? So . . . how are things? Been enjoying the apocalypse?'

Quint frowns. 'No, Dirk. I don't.'

Dirk laughs – he has a high-pitched little giggle-squeal that you'd never expect to come out of this bruising kid who looks like a thirty-eight-year-old man. 'Well, that's too bad,' he says. 'You can make me one later.'

Quint shoots me a look. A look that says, 'Jack, I'm going to strangle you with your shoelaces.'

'So what are you guys doing out here?' Dirk asks. 'Looking for a place to play dolls?'

'No,' I say, 'Although I do have a serious thing for Malibu Barbie. She's just so beachy and wholesome . . .'

Quint rolls his eyes. 'We're looking for June Del Toro. Jack has a bug in his butt about finding her.'

'Well, she's not at her house,' Dirk says.

Wait, what?! My heart starts pounding. What does Dirk know?!

'I saw her a few weeks back, at the Food Frenzy, looking for grub. At least, I think it was her,' Dirk continues.

My face goes hot and I spin around in the seat. 'Well, did you help her!? You helped her, right? No, no, you didn't, did you?! Why didn't you help her??'

Dirk glares at me. 'Relax yourself. Didn't have the chance. She left before I could get to her.'

'But she's alive! And she's in town!' I look at Quint. 'I TOLD YOU SO! PA-POW! IN YO FACE, QUINT!'

Quint frowns. 'Or she WAS alive, a few weeks ago . . .'

'Quint, don't be a negatron. We're making progress here!'

I sit back in the seat and close my eyes.

I can just picture her, curled up, terrified, surrounded by monsters. That's probably definitely what's happening right now . . .

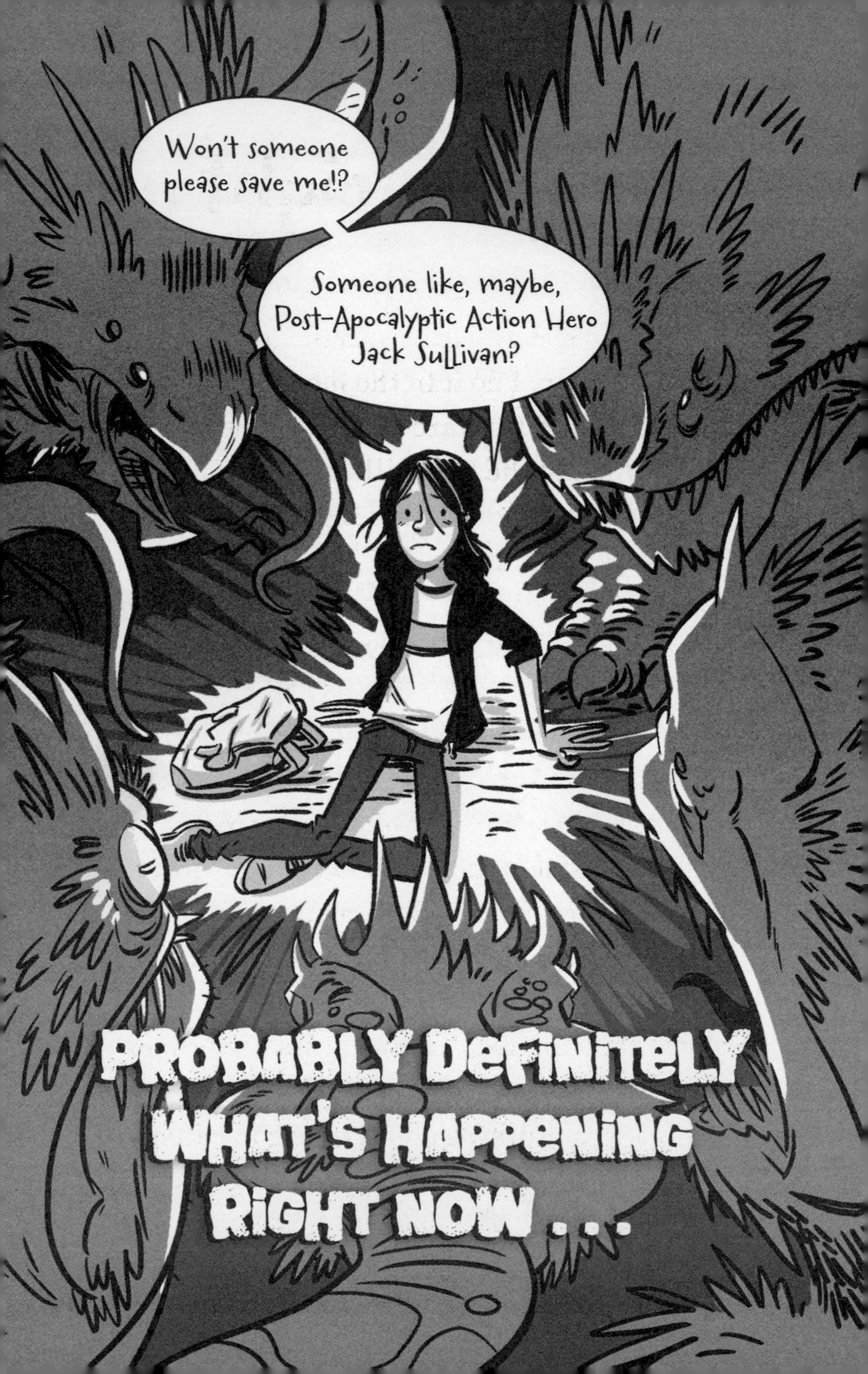
Won't someone please save me!?
Someone like, maybe, Post-Apocalyptic Action Hero Jack Sullivan?
PROBABLY DEFINITELY WHAT'S HAPPENING RIGHT NOW . . .

chapter eight

Every single day now, I drive around town, blaring
Big Mama's horn. I do it in the morning, alone,
before Quint and Dirk are awake. And every few
blocks I whip out the big bullhorn –

'June Del Toro! Are you out there? June Del
Toro! Can you hear me?'

No luck.

It's starting to feel like a wild-goose chase. Or
a wild-June chase.

Today I drive past 12th Street. Which reminds
me – it's almost August 12th. Quint's birthday!

I've never planned a birthday party before.
That's what moms and dads and girls are for. So,
a lot of pressure here. Can't junk this up.

A party should be big and crowded, so that the
birthday person feels admired, appreciated and
accepted. I mean, that's how I always see them
in the movies and on TV and stuff.

So . . . I was thinking about trying to catch a
bunch of the zombies and do something like
this . . .

Eh, scratch that. I'll continue thinking . . .

Rover is awesome.

I always wanted a dog, but when you're a foster kid who's always bounced around, you don't get things like dogs. You might land with a family that has a dog, but you start playing with it and having a blast and next thing you know – off to a new family and no more dog.

But now I've got my own dog – a monster dog.

I'm trying to teach it tricks.

It's going so-so.

Hmm. 'How about play dead!'

Quint shuffles over and interrupts our games.
His eyes are bloodshot and there are big bags
beneath them. I don't think he's slept in days.

He hands me a piece of paper. 'It's a shopping
list. We need everything on it, OK?'

The list is full of bungee cords and metal tubes
and rope and all sorts of junk.

'What's all this for?' I ask.

Quint grins his weirdo grin. 'Inventive
purposes. But trust me, Jack, you'll like it.'

I'll need to go to the hardware store for this.
That's a journey. I climb up into the tree house.

Dirk is in the corner, reading a Hulk comic.

'Let me know if you need help with any of the big words,' I say.

Dirk scowls. 'What do you want?'

'We've got stuff to get,' I say. 'C'mon.'

Dirk shakes his head, groans – but he gets up. He throws on his old grey sweatshirt, pulls on his monster-bashing gloves, and follows me down out of the tree house.

He stomps over to Quint, who's sitting at the picnic table, going over some blueprints.

'Hey, goober,' Dirk barks. 'How come we gotta go get all this stuff for you? Why don't *you* go get it?'

Quint says matter-of-factly, 'Because I'm more valuable here.'

'You think you're more valuable than me, huh?' Dirk says.

'No, I said I'm more valuable *here*. Similar sentences, but they mean very different –'

'I'll show you mean –' Dirk starts.

Quint holds up his hand. 'Dirk, you have no reason to be angry at me. You clearly have some sort of chip on your shoulder, and –'

'Wait, he does?' I look at Dirk. 'Is it a chocolate chip?'

Quint rolls his yes. 'Jack . . .'

I stand on my tippy-toes and examine Dirk's shoulder. 'Or is it a sour cream and onion chip? Either way, I'll eat the chip. I mean, even if it's salt and vinegar.'

'IT'S NOT AN EDIBLE CHIP ON HIS SHOULDER, JACK! It's just a dumb saying.'

'Well, Quint, your dumb saying now has me hungry for chips. That's your fault. Soooo . . . I think you should cook dinner tonight.'

Quint glares at me, hard, like he's trying to laser beam his way through my eyeballs.

'And if you cook us dinner,' I say, 'Dirk will agree not to be a jerk. Right, Dirk?'

You see how I did that? I'm kind of a master of mediation.

Dirk glares at me for a moment, then he looks to Quint. 'Just tell me the real reason you won't go out there.'

Quint shrugs. 'I'm scared.'

Dirk eyes Quint, then says, 'Well, at least you're honest.'

With that, Dirk and I head for Big Mama.

'Do try to get chips, though!' Quint calls after us. 'Now I'm in the mood for chips, too.'

The hardware store parking lot is zombie central. Undead construction-type dudes and undead Home Depot employees stumble around, moaning, eager to eat any breathing human who gets close.

But I'm ready for that. I brought the Scream Machine.

The Scream Machine is DOPENESS DEFINED. Quint and I built it a couple of weeks back.

We pulled an all-nighter, hopped-up on Moonshine Mountain Dew and past-expiration-date Sour Patch Kids, watching horror movies.

Quint recorded all the scenes with people screaming, then transferred the audio to his mom's old iPhone. We attached the iPhone to a loudspeaker and we attached that to an egg timer.

– The Scream Machine –

You place the Scream Machine somewhere, spin the little timer wheel, and when the time is up, the speaker blasts screams at maximum decibels. That brings the zombies a-stumbling, thinking the screaming belongs to some unfortunate, still-living humans.

At the rear of the parking lot, I set the timer to two minutes and drop the Scream Machine out the window. When it goes off – oh man, it sounds like you-know-what-on-Earth:

AIIIIIEEEEEEEEEEEEE!!!!!!

There's a mass zombie migration, leaving
Dirk and me an open path to the store entrance.
We step inside.

We grab a cart. Dirk is dedicated, tracking
down everything on the list. I'm less dedicated
and go straight for the power tools. I spend ten
minutes weighing the pluses and minuses of a
variety of crazy-cool drills. We're heading for
the exit when I spot it.

IT.

Something awesome. Something heavenly.

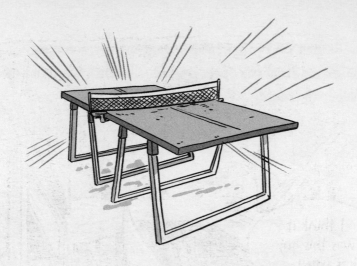

'Dirk!' I say. 'We need that Ping-Pong table. THAT'S what I'll get Quint for his birthday!'

I expect Dirk to tell me that's a dumb idea and that I'm a dumb dork and yadda yadda yadda dork dumb dork, but instead his eyes light up and he says, 'I love Ping-Pong!'

'Who doesn't?! You'd have to be some sort of fun-hating demon to not like Ping-Pong.'

We're stepping closer to the table when Dirk stops. He sniffs at the air. Then he says, 'Jack, have you not been wearing deodorant?'

'I don't think I need to yet –' I start.

'You smell rank,' Dirk says.

Then we both smell it. It is not my pits. It is a foul, fetid, nose-assaulting stench – mould mixed with fresh death.

Dirk and I spin around, and –

I'm scared. Beyond scared. Scared to the second power. Scared squared.

'Dirk,' I whisper. 'I fought this guy before. You see that scar on his forehead? I gave that to him. Then I saw him later, a few blocks from the tree house. I think he's been, like, hunting me.'

'Real great, Jack,' Dirk says. 'Real great.'

'Also, just FYI, his name is Blarg,' I whisper.

'Why is his name –'

Oh.

Blarg doesn't just terrify tiny humans like me – he freaks out zombies, too. In seconds, they're rushing past us, moving toward the door – a whole mess of stumbling, bumbling, stomach-grumbling zombies.

That's when Dirk says it. A sentence I thought I would never ever hear.

'Huh?'

Before I can react, Dirk is lunging past me and grabbing the table – which must weigh a hundred pounds.

'Follow me!' he shouts.

PING-PONG POWER ESCAPE!

119

Dirk and I burst out into the parking lot. The Scream Machine is still howling away.

Dirk shoves the Ping-Pong table and all of Quint's junk in the back of Big Mama while I clamber up into the driver's seat. Dirk hops in, yelling, 'Go, go, go!'

Behind us, Blarg bursts out through the front of the store, bringing down the walls. It's about as loud as a marching band falling off a cliff. Blarg's like a tank, crushing cars and stomping shopping carts beneath his feet.

'That thing is gonna kill us!' Dirk yells. For the first time, Dirk sounds scared. Whaddya know. He's human after all.

'Don't worry,' I say. 'Big Mama is prepared for a situation like this . . .'

I reach down to the control panel and flick the switch marked BUTTER-SLICK SLINGERS.

SHOOONT! SHOOONT!

Blarg takes his next step, and – **SLIP!**

His feet go out. He grabs for a streetlight, trying to brace himself, but – **SNAP!** It cracks in two, and –

CRASH!

Big Mama: 1

Blarg: 0

As we race away, I glance at the rear-view mirror.

Blarg's eyes. His many eyes. They're watching us. They're watching *me*. ME! Hating me. Promising revenge. I have this horrible feeling that I'll be meeting this vile villain again.

'Uh . . . this car has butter slicks?' Dirk asks, snapping me out of my Blarg-induced terror.

I nod. 'Yep. Pretty rad, right? Quint's idea. We had to haul four barrels of the stuff from the movie theatre, but it was worth it.'

'Those butter slicks saved our butts,'
Dirk says.

I nod. Quint's good at saving butts. Saved
mine many times. He's a primo butt-saver.

Dirk is quiet for a moment. At last, he says,
'Maybe I don't give that kid enough credit . . .'

———————

When we get back to the tree house, Quint is
in the midst of having a full-blown freak out.

'What took you so long?' he screams.
'I thought you were zombie chow!'

'We ran into some trouble,' I say.

Quint frowns.

'Don't worry,' I say. 'After we ran *into* it,
we ran *away* from it.'

'I got you a birthday present,' Dirk says.

'What, Dirk? Noogies? A punch in the nose?'

'No, for serious. But not just from me. From
me and Jack. The two of us. Happy birthday,
geek,' Dirk says, reaching into the back of
Big Mama and unveiling our super-awesome
new Ping-Pong table (which also makes a good
makeshift battering ram, as we learned).

Quint's eyes light up.

Dirk steps forward and sticks out his hand. Quint flinches. Sort of stumbles back, like he thinks it's a trap.

Dirk rolls his eyes. Quint stops himself.

He stands up straight – straighter than I've ever seen. Then he steps forward and shakes Dirk's hand.

See? Ping-Pong solves all problems.

chapter nine

After our little birthday celebration,
I tell Quint all about the monster Blarg,
and Quint FREAKS.

I tell Quint to stop being a nuclear-
overreactor, but secretly, I'm glad Quint
knows about the Blarg threat.

Quint puts his current top-secret project
on hold, the one we went to Home Depot to get
supplies for, until we finish truly arming the
tree house. He has Dirk knock down the back
wall to the Robinsons' garage, so we can get
inside without opening it up to the street side of
the house. And inside the garage, Quint sets up
a full-blown invention workshop . . .

Razor Frisbees.

Explosive football launcher.

Spring shoes.

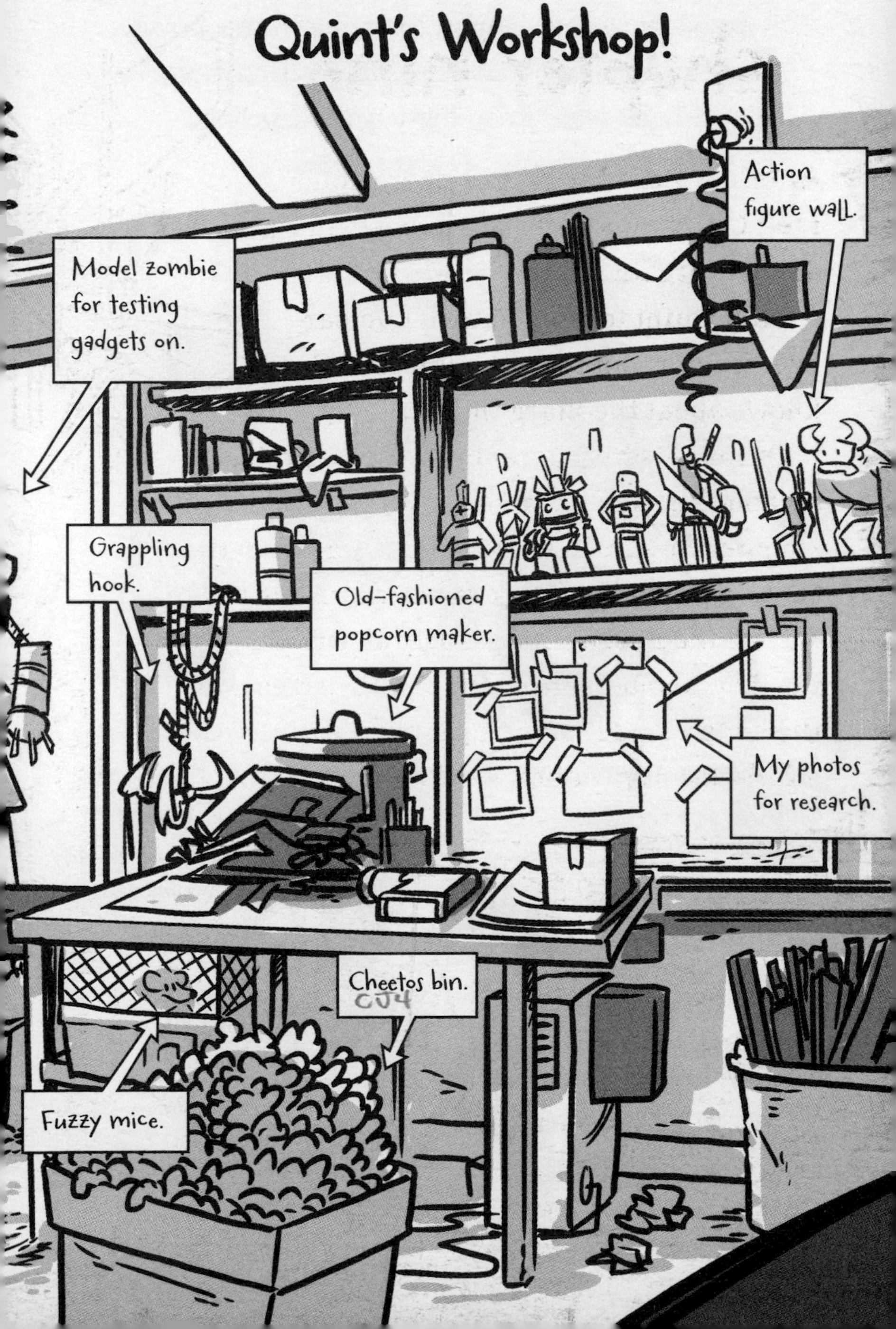

Quint's Workshop!
Model zombie for testing gadgets on.
Action figure wall.
Grappling hook.
Old-fashioned popcorn maker.
My photos for research.
Cheetos bin.
Fuzzy mice.

So while Quint spends his time in the garage, working on blueprints for a newly fortified tree house, Dirk and I keep busy and time flies . . . I take more photos. *Great photos.*

Some afternoons, Dirk and I just go out and look for trouble.

Every few days, Quint hands Dirk and me a
list of things we need to help arm and defend the
tree house. It's easy – the town is a smorgasbord!
All for the taking! Fireworks, video games,
trampolines – everything.

Dirk spray-paints a giant, almost life-size
version of Blarg on the side of the neighbours'
house. Quint says I need to be prepared, so the
next time I see Blarg, it's the last time – and not
the last time I see him because he plucks my
eyeballs out or something, but the last time I see
him 'cause I slay him.

Remember how I said I look at things like video games? Well, if life is a video game now, it sure feels like Blarg is the final boss. And everyone knows you NEVER battle the final boss without being prepared.

I sit and stare at that big painting on the side of the house. And I look at that forehead. The scar.

What did Arnold say, in that movie with the alien?

So while I spend my time practising whacking away at spray-paint Blarg, Dirk finishes digging the moat – which is really just a swimming pool that goes all the way around the tree house. We had to wait for heavy rain to fill the pool. It's pretty muddy, but still – it's our own moat pool!

Whenever Quint takes a break from his plotting and planning, we play swimming pool games. Like diving-board catch.

Quint and I are terrible at diving-board catch. I haven't caught a single ball yet. Something goes wrong every time: either I jump too high or he throws it in the wrong direction.

And still, every morning and every evening, I hop into Big Mama and go for my ride – cruising down the street, hollering 'June Del Toro! Are you out there? June Del Toro! Are you out there?!'

Still nothing.

But I'm not giving up hope.

So anyway, yeah, this is it – this is life now.

And on a random night, when the weather is right, Quint and Dirk and I do something different.

We stop.

We stop adventuring and we stop researching and we stop battling monsters and we just chill out. We make root beer cocktails and we roast marshmallows and we kick back, relax and enjoy the post-apocalyptic sunset.

Just me and my best friends, hanging out in the tree house at the end of the world.

And – oh, yeah – this puppy is seriously armed to the teeth.

Catapult #1.

Zip line (great for last-minute escapes. Also for drying socks).

Cool guy.

Mountain Dew distillery (working on perfecting the formula – currently just hot dog water and green food colouring).

Toilet bucket.

The Tree House at the End of the World

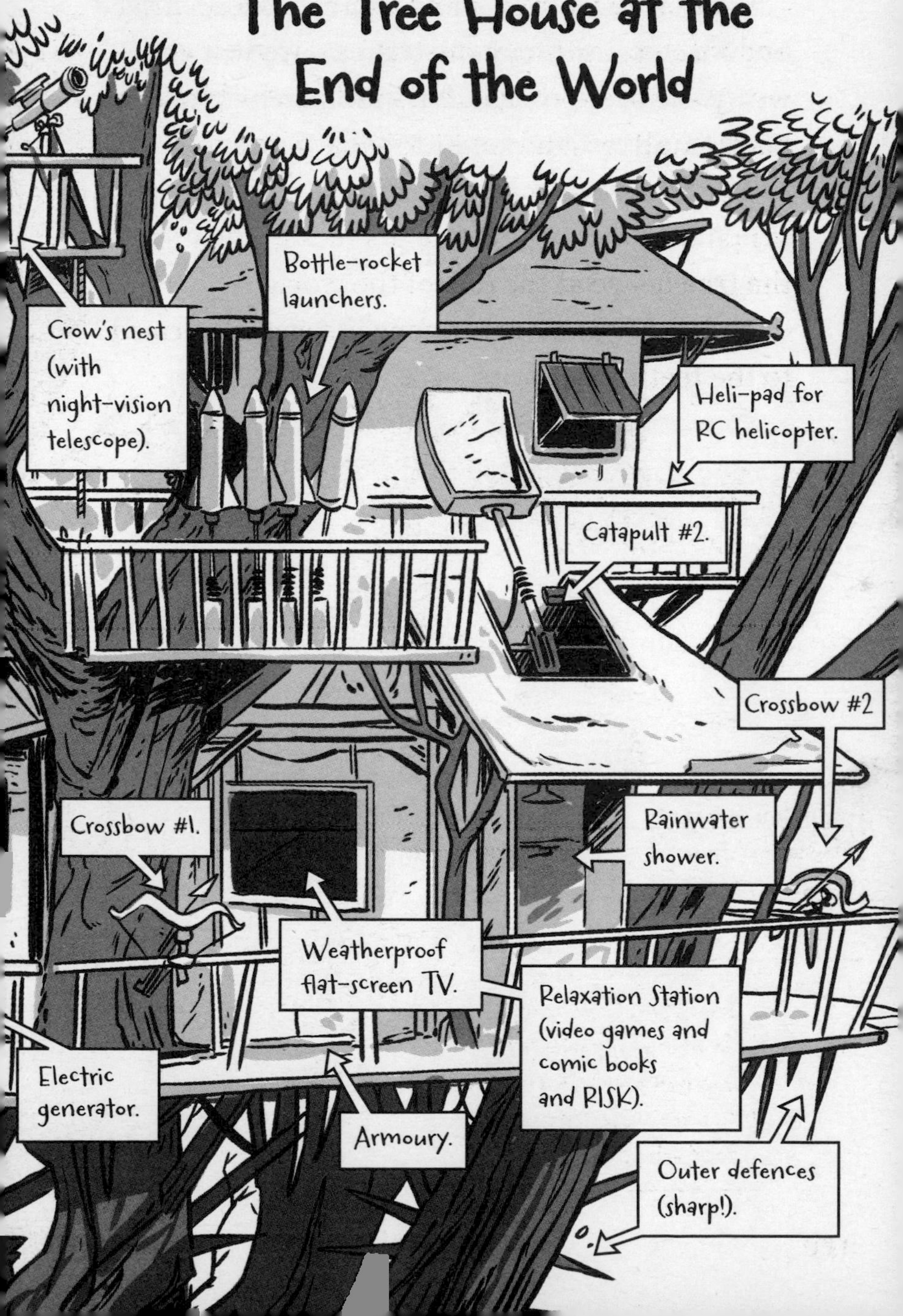

Crow's nest (with night-vision telescope).
Bottle-rocket launchers.
Heli-pad for RC helicopter.
Catapult #2.
Crossbow #2
Crossbow #1.
Rainwater shower.
Weatherproof flat-screen TV.
Relaxation Station (video games and comic books and RISK).
Electric generator.
Armoury.
Outer defences (sharp!).

But don't forget – I know all about being jerked out of good situations. As soon as anything in my life ever gets good, it quickly changes. Something cruddy comes to take it away.

And I suspect I know what that 'something cruddy' is.

Blarg.

My Spidey sense is tingling. A buzzing in the back of my brain, telling me that the nightmarish monster is growing tired of waiting for me. That soon enough, Blarg will come to finish me off . . .

chapter ten

It's early afternoon and I've eaten all the donuts when Quint and Dirk finally come out of the garage, ready to reveal this top-secret Home Depot supply project thing. Dirk is carrying a contraption made of bungee cords and ropes and an old Harley-Davidson motorcycle seat we yanked off my zombified neighbour's bike.

'Um . . . what is that?' I ask.

'What the huh?' I say.

Quint whistles and Rover bolts over. Dirk begins placing the thing on his back.

I can't believe what I'm seeing: it's a saddle. A saddle for riding Rover.

If this thing works, Rover will no longer just be a goofy monster that hangs around and sort of almost does tricks.

Saddle.

He'll be . . .

- The Beast -

Reins, for steering.

Gleeful puppy-dog grin.

And just like that, Rover is off! I grab the
reins and my pet monster stampedes across the
yard like a runaway bronco.

'Uh . . . dudes?!?' I shout, but it's too late . . .

Rover barrels right through the backyard
fence and out into the street.

But Rover only goes faster. He rampages
down Prescott Street, crashing through fences,
charging across backyards, smashing down
front doors and tearing through houses.

As Rover veers toward the town forest, I spot
a dangling mass of Vine-Thingies ahead of us.

Snaking plants, reaching out, eager, ready to choke me the instant I get close.

I manage to pull the Louisville Slicer out from its sheath just in time, and I swing –

We dash past the man-eating plant monsters, and Rover leads us up a tree-lined path to the top of Bear Hill, the highest point in town.

Rover slows to a trot.

'I just need to teach you how to stop, buddy,' I say, scratching Rover's ears as I take a look around. You can see everything from Bear Hill.

I see the comic book store.

I see the high school football field.

I see the middle school, and I –

The middle school.

I squint. There's something hanging from one of the windows. I yank out my camera and zoom in.

A sweatshirt. I know that sweatshirt.

That's June Del Toro's sweatshirt!

That means . . .

She must still be in the school! She must not have left, after the craziness in the parking lot! She must be trapped in there – either someplace inside where she can't hear me calling or someplace she can't respond from.

Holy moo cows. This is it.

THIS IS IT!

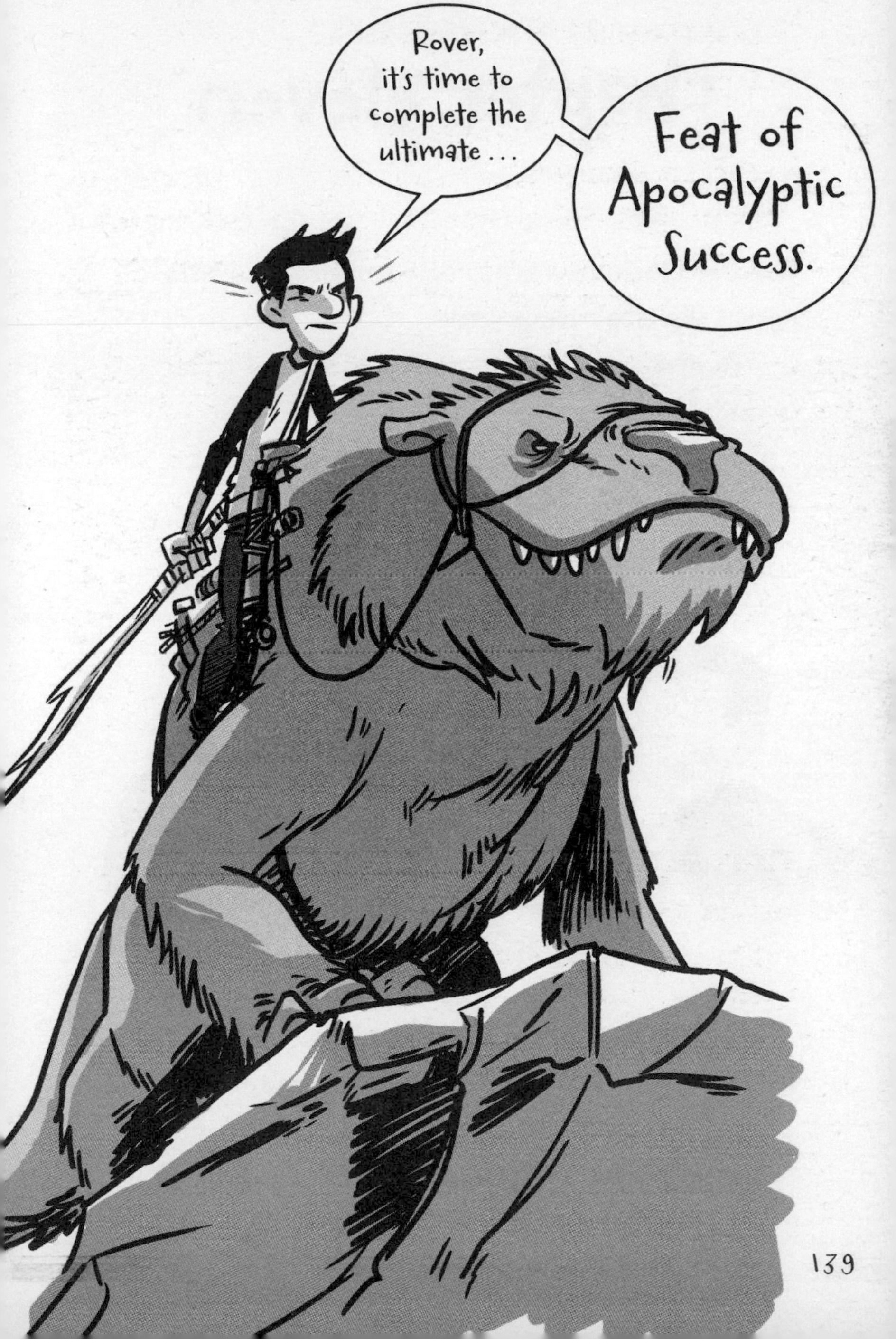
Rover, it's time to complete the ultimate . . .
Feat of Apocalyptic Success.

chapter eleven

Neither Quint or Dirk really understand this need I have to rescue June.

'We just have to!' I say. 'It's the right thing to do.'

Quint rolls his eyes, and leans over –

Argh!

I say yes just to shut them up, and then we all agree – we'll go to the school to rescue June.

We gather around the big map in the command centre to plot a route across town. After some intense debate, we agree on:

1. Down South Street, past the Dozer zone.

2. Across the Old Bridge, where the Octo-Beast lives (DRIVE FAST HERE!).

3. Around the quarry, where the Stone Tower Monster hangs out.

4. Straight down Main Street, which requires serious driving skills to navigate all the abandoned old cars and undeaders.

5. Up Spring Street to Parker Middle School, where we race inside and I say, 'JUNE, I'M HERE TO RESCUE YOU! COME WITH ME IF YOU WANT TO LIVE!' and June says, 'OH, THANK YOU, JACK SULLIVAN! YOU ARE AN AMAZING HERO!'

6. Hop back into Big Mama and cruise back to the tree house, pumping summertime hero jams.

7. Live happily ever after, slaying monsters and living the good life.

We all pretty much agree –

Good plan.

Great plan!

Best plan anybody ever had in the history of plans!

But what to do about Rover?

Quint's been working on building him a little Snoopy-style doghouse (monsterhouse?), where Rover can sleep and play with his bone.

Dozer pinky bone.

Chomp, chomp, slurp...

But the monsterhouse isn't done yet. So I say to Rover (like he can understand me ...), 'Rover, I have to go do something very important. Post-Apocalyptic Action Hero business. You stay here. And for once, DON'T FOLLOW!'

Rover makes a super-sad puppy-monster face.

'Don't you make that face at me, Rover,' I say. 'We'll be back in two shakes of a monster's tail.'

Inside Big Mama, I wrap my fingers around the leather wheel.

I can't believe it. It's happening. The moment I've been waiting for. The opportunity to truly be Jack Sullivan, Post-Apocalyptic Action Hero. It's here. And this is it – the big one ...

THE RIDE THROUGH MONSTER LAND TO RESCUE JUNE!

At the Old Bridge, I gun it past the Octo-Beast.
The Octo-Beast bursts out of the water, flinging his
slimy tentacles around! Our bottle-rocket launchers
don't fail us –

At the quarry I burn rubber, pedal to the metal,
racing right beneath the giant Stone Tower Monster.

I don't think he's too bright . . .

Up Main Street, I do my best not to slam into every single parked car. I take out six bicycles, two stop signs and a really nice BMW.

Not bad for a high-speed cruise!

Racing around the corner of Summer Street, I see it.

Our goal.

Parker Middle School! And . . . yikes.

LOTS OF ZOMBIES!

I steer Big Mama up over the sidewalk. Laying on the brakes, the truck slides, spinning around 180 degrees, tearing up grass and SLAMMING into the big old oak tree in front of the school.

We're within spitting distance of the school. We can worry about getting Big Mama free when we leave.

'Rescue time!' I shout.

We scramble out of the truck and race up the school's front steps. I grab hold, and – *clink!*

It's locked! I look back at Big Mama. Zombies are coming from every direction. Surrounding it and surrounding us.

It's a swarm!

Now we have no way of escaping and no way of getting into the school.

This may *not* have been the 'best plan anybody ever had in the history of plans'.

I squeeze the handle and give it everything I've got. But the door won't budge. Blast! Blast my pathetic little arms!

Quint scratches his chin. 'If I could fashion an electrical charge, I could blow the door off its hinges. But that would take at least –'

RIP!!!

'Yeah, well, I loosened it for you,' I mutter as I step inside Parker Middle School. There's a *KA-KLANG* as Dirk jams the door back into place behind us.

Now, here's the thing with schools. I hate them. You probably do, too. Most kids hate school. But I hate school **WAY MORE** than most kids. See, I've attended about ten different schools in my thirteen years. Every year, shuffled from one place to the next, every time a new home, a new school to go with it.

To me, every time I enter a school, it's a reminder of how I'm not normal. How I'm not like other, regular people. How I just *don't fit in.*

And seriously, again, like I said – if you think I'm trying to get sympathy points or something, I'm totally not. I'm just saying – as much as you hate school, I hate it like 88 times as much.

So when I stepped into the school and saw it had been ravaged and nearly destroyed, I was surprised that I felt, well, sad.

But I think I know why. See, this school is where I met Quint. The best friend I ever had – and even though I've known him for less than a year, it's the longest friendship I've ever had too.

And this is where I met Dirk. Big, lovable, jerk-faced, reformed-bully Dirk.

And June.

June, who is somewhere in this building, trapped, in danger, possibly wounded, in desperate need of our help. June, who doesn't really like me. June, who I'm trying to save anyway.

As we step farther into the school, it gets darker. Soon we can barely see anything.

Quint reaches into his bag and pulls out this little headlamp thing because of course Quint owns something like that. Which I'm not knocking, 'cause it's actually pretty great.

Quint's headlamp lights up and we see –

Nothing.

It's empty. Abandoned. Scraps of paper litter the floor. Flyers for school dances that should

have happened months ago. No zombies,
no monsters, no nothing.

It's quiet.

As action heroes like myself say, **too quiet**.

Our footsteps echo as we tiptoe through
the halls. Past the empty music room. Past
the empty principal's office. Past the empty
auditorium.

Two more turns, and we come out at the
school's long rear hallway. I look down the hall.
It's a mess – backpacks on the ground, lockers
hanging open. But no zombies.

All of it, empty.

And then I hear it.

Y'know when you're bowling, and you throw
a gutter ball? It's that sound – that sound,
combined with the ghastly undead howl of
hungry zombies, coming from the darkness.

'Quint,' I say. 'Pass me your headlamp.'

'What?!? This is mine. Get your own, friend!'
he says, all offended.

I groan and yank the thing off his head. I
shine the light down the hall behind us, looking
to see what horrible thing could be chasing us.
And when I see it, it's just ... it's –

FEAR.

Fear unlike anything I've ever known.
Not just fear of death, but fear of the cause of
death. Fear of this hideous, disgusting evil
upon us.

I'm too scared to speak. I just sort of push
Quint and shove Dirk. Ushering them forward,
until we're all running, full-sprint, down the
hallway.

'JUST KEEP MOVING.'
'WHAT IS IT, JACK?' Dirk demands.
'It's a –'

ZOMBIE BALL!

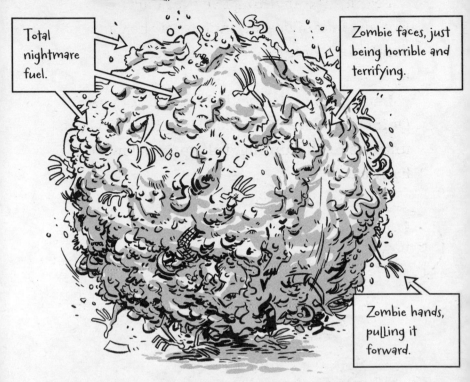

Total nightmare fuel.

Zombie faces, just being horrible and terrifying.

Zombie hands, pulling it forward.

It is a ball. A massive ball. A massive ball of tangled limbs. A massive ball of tangled zombie limbs: all of them wrapped together, legs and arms and bodies intertwined. Faces, hands, feet, legs – everything knotted and twisted.

Their hands are reaching, grabbing, pulling them along so that the ball is barrelling down the hallway toward us. This rolling mass of undead bodies fills the hallway completely, offering no hope of hiding or dodging.

151

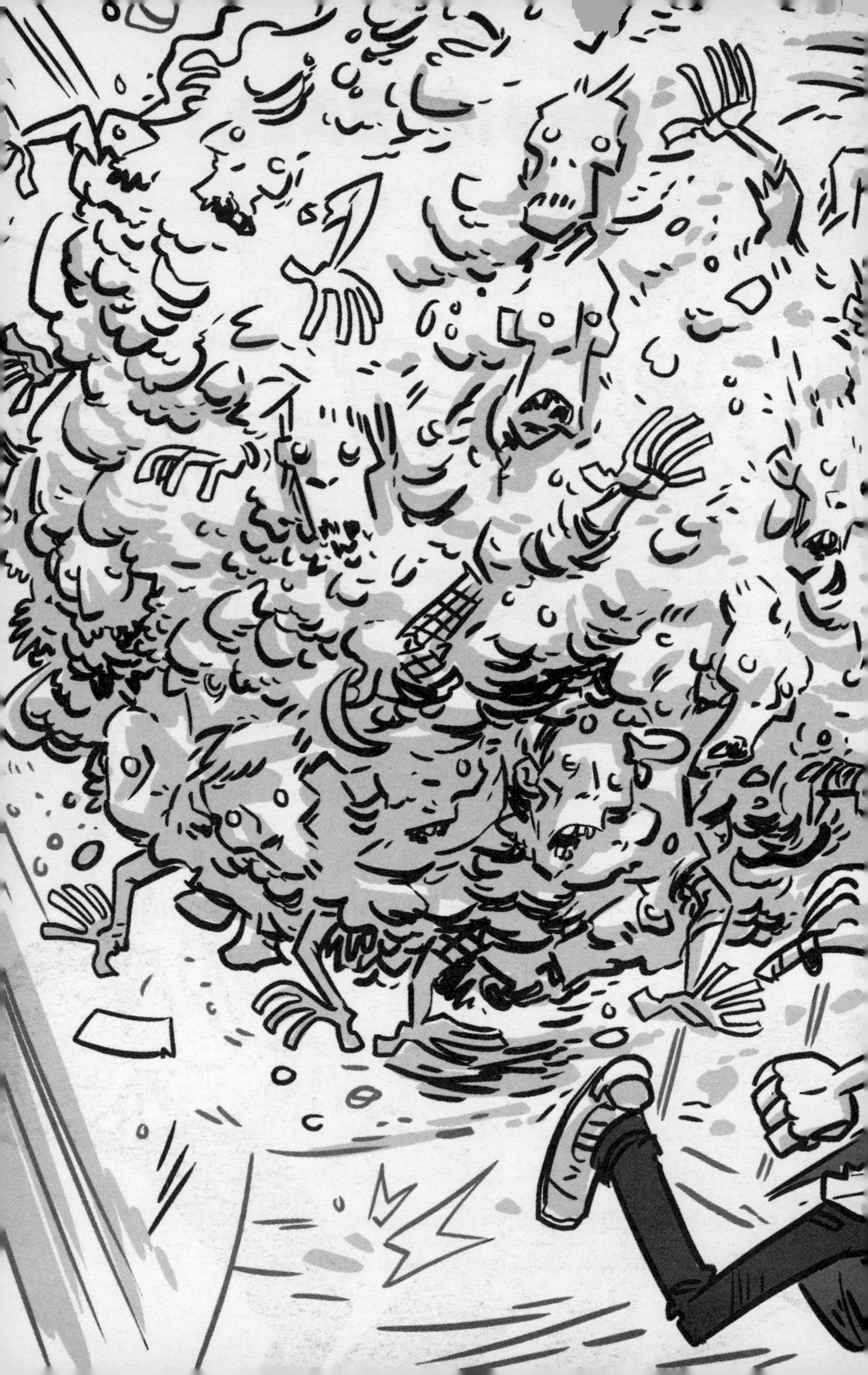

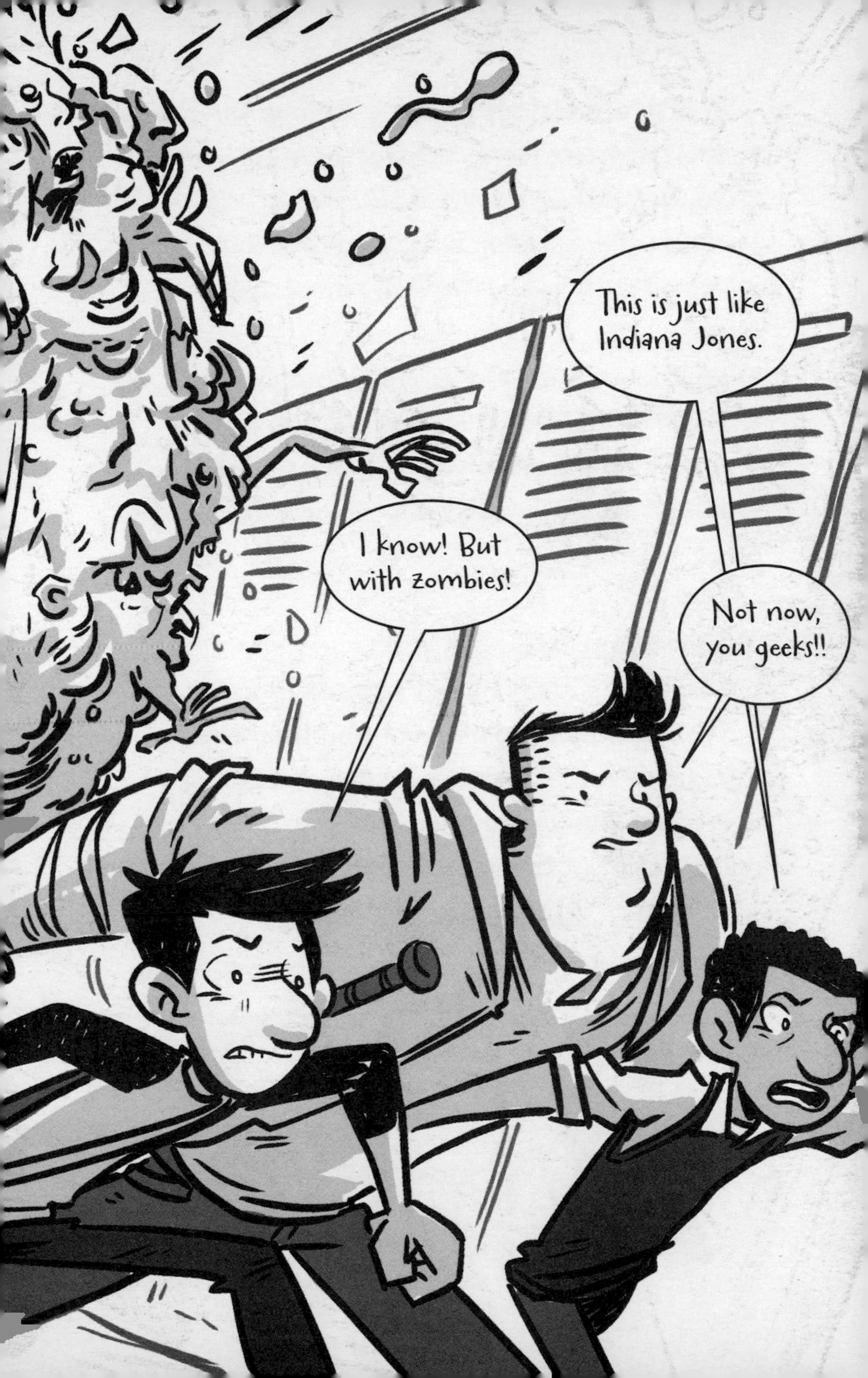
This is just like Indiana Jones.
I know! But with zombies!
Not now, you geeks!!

We rip around the corner, then up the stairs to the 7th grade floor, taking the steps two at a time. But THE ZOMBIE BALL FOLLOWS US! It barrels up the stairs, bony hands grabbing each step and pulling the undead monstrosity ever closer.

We race around the corner, into the hall, and – HOLY MOTHER OF CRUD BALLS!

A set of double doors ahead of us. Dirk grabs hold and tugs. No use. They're locked from the other side.

I turn.

The zombie ball is upon us.

This is it. This is how it's gonna end.

We're gonna be crushed – and then eaten – by a giant ball of twisted, entangled zombies!

We're doomed. Doomed to die at the many, many hands of the zombie ball.

About-to-die faces!

KLIK-KLAK!

Suddenly, the doors are open! We're stumbling back, through the doorway, tumbling to the floor.

A strict voice orders us to 'GET BACK!'

I crawl down the hall, away from the rapidly approaching ball o' death, then – *BANG!* – the double doors slam shut and a lock goes *KLINK* just as –

ZOMBIE BALL BUSTED!

'Wha– What happened?' Quint says.

'Who opened the doors?' Dirk asks.

I think I know the answer . . .

I stand up, shining the headlamp. And there she is. A figure stepping out of the darkness.

The girl I came to rescue.

The damsel in distress.

June Del Toro.

What are you fools doing here?

chapter twelve

June looks like some sort of crazed killer Amazonian warrior princess! She's got a broom handle carved into a spear and her hair is whipping around like there's a breeze but there's no breeze, it's just her hair being, like, wicked.

I'd had a few different ideas about how this rescue might go down.

Most of them looked something like this:

But none of them looked like this . . . what's happening now –

'But we're here to rescue you!' I say.

'I don't need rescuing,' June says coolly.

'Of course you do!' I exclaim. 'You're trapped here! I knew it 'cause I saw your sweatshirt in the window. The red one with the yellow stripes!'

June looks at me like I'm a creeper. 'You know what *clothes* I own?'

Guess I do sound like a creeper. 'Um, I just pay attention to those things, I guess . . .' I mumble. 'I'm, ah, observant.'

June frowns. 'That's a little cute and a little weird. But I don't need help.'

'Jack,' she says, 'my parents are coming to rescue me. All I need to do is wait here. What I don't need is three idiot boys running around, bringing zombie balls upstairs. Understand?'

'How do you know your parents are coming?'

'I just know, OK?' she says, her voice harsh.

'Look, June, I don't think you understand. You're probably in shock. See, I am pretty, pretty awesome. I'm like a post-apocalyptic James Bond. I mean, I've got a licence to kill monsters.'

June looks at me like she's going to feed me to the zombies herself.

'No, for real, I do. See?' I say, handing June a piece of paper.

She takes the paper, eyes it suspiciously, then looks up and says, 'Jack, this is a torn-off piece of a fast-food menu that you wrote "Jack Sullivan, Licence to Kill Monsters" on.'

I cross my arms, lean against a locker, and smile like a boss. 'Yup. Sick, right? You should feel honoured that I'm here to rescue you.'

June is less than impressed. 'You spelled "licence" wrong.'

I shrug. 'Spelling doesn't matter when it comes to killing monsters.'

'Yeah, but killing *does* matter. And you spelled

"kill" wrong, too. You used three *L*s.'

'That's on purpose. The extra L is for extra monster killing.'

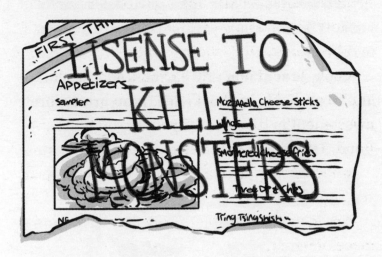

'JACK! I DON'T NEED RESCUING!'

Whoa. Dirk, Quint and I exchange freaked-out glances. Angry girls are more terrifying than any beasts.

After a moment, June catches her breath. 'Look, Jack, guys, thank you for coming here. Glad to know other people are alive. But I don't need rescuing, and, really, I'd like you to leave. Please.'

I take a step back. I don't understand – I've come this far. I've searched high and low for June. And now that I've finally found her – she has no interest in being rescued?!

No. Doesn't compute.

I need a new tactic. I need to buy some time to convince her of my awesomeness . . .

'Can we at least stay here until morning?' I ask. 'Y'know, since we just busted our butts to get here.'

June glares at me. After a moment she shakes her broom-handle spear with frustration and says, 'FINE!'

'Great!' I say. 'So . . .'

And with that, we begin a . . .

DOIN'-DANGEROUS-STUFF-IN-THE-SCHOOL MONTAGE!

When we're done, I collapse on the floor, wipe the sweat from my eyes and pull out my Feats of Apocalyptic Success list. I just completed a few big ones, so I start checking them off.

Suddenly, June's standing over me. 'Gimme that,' she says, yanking the paper from my hands. She reads it out loud. '"Punch a zombie in the nose: 10 points. Tie a balloon to a Dozer: 50 points. Hit a Dozer in the butt with a paintball: 50 points. Swing from a vine like Indiana Jones: 80 points. Evade Principal Zombie: 100 points."'

She lowers the paper. 'You did all this stuff?'

'Yup!' I say, grinning. 'That vine one was tough. Harrison Ford makes it look so easy, but really, you have to get a good grip and make sure it's not, like, a weak vine and make sure the water's deep enough and if there are, like, bees anywhere, then no way –'

'Jack, wait – are you, um, are you actually having fun during the end of the world?'

'I mean – look, it's terrible,' I say, all serious now. 'But I'm not gonna just give up. Some days are way scary, yeah. And sometimes things are pretty freaking sad. But I'm trying real, real hard here to keep on living and enjoying every moment. With friends.'

June looks down at the paper. "Damsel in Distress," she reads. 'What's that one?'

Uh-oh. *Bustedddd*. 'Um, well – that's the big one. That's rescuing you.'

June half-smiles, leans against the locker, and slides down until she plops onto her butt.

She's staring off down the hall, watching Quint chase Dirk with a mop and bucket. Dirk is laughing – that goofy, high-pitched squeal he has.

'Gotcha! You're it!'

June looks back to me. 'You guys are a little nuts, you know that?'

I grin. 'Being a little nuts is a little good, I think.'

June shifts uncomfortably, like she's thinking about something real hard. I think this is it. She's going to see the light. She's going to realize, like I realized, that life during the Monster Apocalypse is a whole brick-load better with buddies.

Then she looks at me. We lock eyes. Just like we locked eyes months ago, in the parking lot, when the world began to collapse. And she says, 'It's late. You should get some sleep. You guys are leaving first thing in the morning.'

Groan.

I round up Dirk and Quint – who were, no joke, in the middle of a tickle fight. June has built a base in our old homeroom by clearing away most of the desks and dragging in the couch from the teachers' lounge.

Quint, Dirk and I head out into the hall to raid lockers and gather jackets and backpacks so we can make little makeshift beds.

When we're out of earshot, Dirk whispers, 'So what's the deal? The girl isn't coming tomorrow?'

'I'm still working on it,' I say.

'We leave tomorrow morning, Jack, no matter what,' Quint says. 'We can't leave Rover.'

'I know, I know,' I say. 'I'm on it, OK? I'm on it. Jack on the case. Gonna be handled.'

Then we all climb into our beds. I toss and turn, mind racing. I'm wide awake. Zero sleep happening. Also, not super helpful that Dirk snores like a grizzly bear suffering from a serious head cold.

How do I get June to see the light?

I hear something then. Not snoring. Something else.

Footsteps.

Oh, no.

During our awesome action school montage, did I mess up – did I leave a door unlocked? Is there a zombie shuffling around the room right now? About to rip into our throats and dine on our delectable neck flesh?

chapter thirteen

I sit up.

Squinting in the darkness, I see a figure, creeping across the room. I hear the door unlock, then watch the figure step out into the hall.

In the dim light, I can make out that it's June.

Hey, I just used 'make out' and 'June' in the same sentence. Go me!

Anyway, what is she up to?

I kick my way out of my jacket-blanket bed and tiptoe out into the hallway. June is pulling open a door and stepping into the stairwell. I know that stairwell. It leads to the roof.

I follow her.

The roof is well-lit by the moon. June is standing near the ledge. Next to her is a large plastic trash barrel.

June spins, startled.

'Sorry. Didn't mean to scare you.'

'You didn't,' she says. That's a lie.

'What are you doing up here? It's four in the morning.'

June reaches into the trash bin and pulls out
a tennis ball. I peek inside the barrel. It's filled
with hundreds of tennis balls. Other empty trash
barrels are scattered across the roof.

'This is how I let out frustration,' June says,
hurling a tennis ball toward the crowd of
zombies below. The tennis ball nails a zombie –
our gym teacher, Mr Perkis – in the back.

'It's a game I play,' June says. 'Ten points for
hitting a zombie in the head, five points for the

body, twenty points if I call it. Like if I say, "Jess
Aronesty, in the head" and I actually hit Jess
Aronesty in the head, that's twenty points.'

'Like my Feats of Apocalyptic Success! Are
you copying me? Don't be a copycat, June,' I say,
grinning.

June laughs. That makes my heart swell.
Great, now I have a swollen heart. I hope the
swelling stops before it kills me.

I reach into the bin. 'OK, I'm calling it.
Mr Winik, in the face,' I say.

I cock back my arm and fling the tennis ball.
I miss Mr Winik by about forty-six and a half
feet. 'Lame,' June says as she reaches down into
the barrel. 'Lame and zero points.'

'I saw you,' I say, 'running inside, when it was happening. And you saw me.'

June nods.

'Our eyeballs,' I say, sounding very suave and European. 'Our eyeballs shared a moment.'

June rolls her eyes in the cutest way possible. 'You are weird, Jack. Annnyyyhoo, yeah, I ran to the newspaper office first. Oh, that reminds me! We were going to put one of your pictures in that issue. The one you took of band practice.'

'Ugh,' I groan. 'That pic was lamer than a one-legged zombie.'

June laughs softly, barely. 'You just wanted to take photos of adventure stuff, right?'

I shrug. 'I'm just an adventuring kind of guy.'

'Well, you got your chance now,' she says with a sigh.

I nod and sigh with her.

'Anyway, yeah, I went inside. I thought I'd wait a little while and then the police would show up and my parents would come get me. Never happened. Zombies came, clawing at the door. I hid in the closet – didn't come out for two whole days. And when I did come out there was . . . just . . . some monster – big as a house! Eating people! And the other people, they were – well, you know.'

'Yep. I know. Undead.'

'So I locked doors and did my best to keep the things trapped downstairs, in the rear of the school. And now it's just me here.'

'What about your parents?'

June gulps and grimaces, like it hurts to swallow. Maybe I shouldn't have asked.

'I saw them on the fifth day,' she says. 'A big bus rolled by, pulled by a tank. There was a soldier on a microphone, saying anyone who was not a zombie should come with them. My parents were in the bus. They were looking out at the school. I banged my fists on the window and I screamed and I shouted until my throat was sore. But it worked. They saw me.'

'Wait – really? They saw you?'

June nods. 'My dad tried to run out. But the soldier wouldn't let him off the bus. And I couldn't go out there without the zombies getting me. Then the bus turned the corner, and they were gone. Just . . . gone.'

I pick at my hangnail, uncomfortable, not sure what to say. 'At least they're safe, somewhere . . .'

June shrugs. After a moment, she says, 'Jack,

I'm sorry I freaked at you guys before. But you see why I can't leave the school. My parents know I'm here. They're going to come for me. And I can't have you guys messing that up.'

'But, June, when your parents come back, everyone will come with them. No matter where you are, they'll find you. Even if you're, y'know, like, maybe, hanging out in my tree house . . .'

June glares at me.

'What!? I'm just saying, I really think you should come back to the tree house with us. It's fun – there's a wind chime, we have cookies sometimes.'

June sighs. She launches a tennis ball. It bounces off the back of an 8th grade chemistry teacher with a *TONK!*

'It's nasty, right?' June says. 'Be honest. The tree house is nasty and smells like boys. Boy smell is worse then zombie smell. Almost.'

I reach into the barrel. 'See the janitor, Mr Urk? I'm going to knock the hat off his head.'

'No way.'

I narrow my eyes. 'Just watch. I'm super accurate.'

I launch the ball. And I miss badly. The tennis

ball hits our assistant principal in the face,
bounces off her, hits some rando in the chest,
then rolls along the ground, where another
zombie steps on it, falls over into another
zombie, and about a dozen of the undead things
collapse in a goofy pile.

I look at June, and suddenly, together –

HA-HA-HA!

'Oh yeah, you're real accurate, Jack,'
June says, trying to catch her breath.

'Hey!' I exclaim. 'I took out like twelve
zombies with that one throw. If we were
bowling, that'd be a strike. Of course, if we
were bowling, we'd be at a bowling alley and
they'd probably have air hockey and that would
be fantastic.'

My sides ache. June says, panting, 'I don't think I've laughed in months.'

I smile at her. 'I'm tellin' ya, June, life is better when you get a chance to laugh every now and then. Even if there's boy smell involved. And let me just say, real quick – I have the BEST boy smell. Top notch, Grade A!'

'Let me guess. Lynx body spray?'

'Even better. Christmas tree air freshener. I rub it all over my chest every morning – it's nice, gets you in that holiday mood.'

June shakes her head and goes quiet again. She shifts uneasily, like she's thinking real hard. She picks at her sneakers. At last, she says, 'OK, tell me about this tree house of yours.'

My eyes go wide and I leap to my feet. My heart is just about pounding out of my chest.

'Jack,' she says, 'you can stop talking now.
I like this, here, what's happening. I like
laughing. I like stupid games. Tomorrow
morning, when you leave, I'll come with you.'

AHHHHHHHHHH!!!!!!!! I can't believe it I
can't believe it I can't believe it.

'OK, sure,' I say, trying real hard to sound like
I don't care. 'That's cool if you want to. I mean,
whatevs. No worries, either way.'

June shakes her head. 'You're a huge dork.'

'Only on opposite day.'

'Just know one thing, Jack.'

'What?'

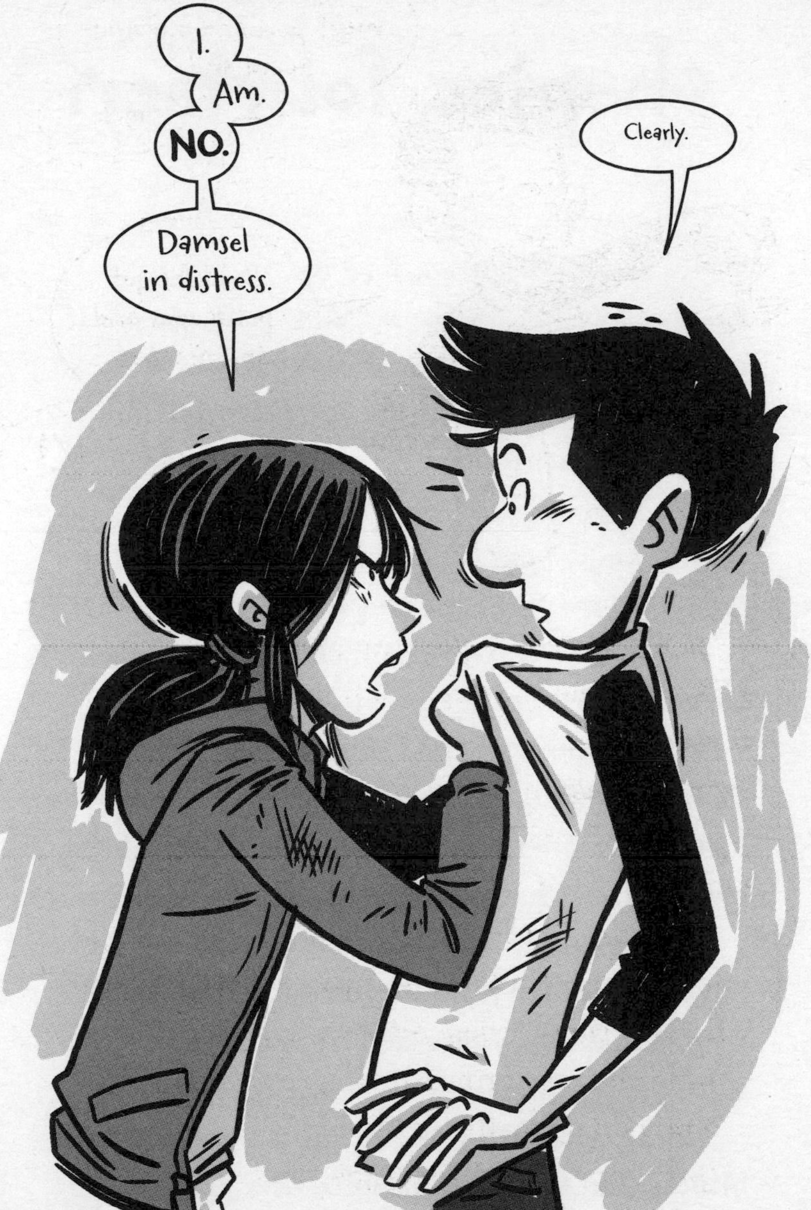
I.
Am.
NO.
Damsel in distress.
Clearly.

chapter fourteen

When June and I step back into Mr Vogel's room, Quint and Dirk are waiting for us. Quint is leaning against the far window with his arms crossed. He looks like a ticked-off teacher who wants to know why it took you thirty minutes to run to the bathroom.

'Uh, hey, buddies,' I say. 'You're awake?'

'You know I can't sleep without my earplugs, Jack. I heard you sneaking out.'

I roll my eyes. 'Oh yes, of course. Your earwax-collecting nuggets . . .'

'They're not earwax-collecting nuggets, Jack! They're earplugs and you know I have sensitive hearing, so I – ugh, never mind. Now that I'm awake, I see that we have a problem.'

'No, we don't!' I exclaim. 'No problems! We have good news! June is coming. Right, June?'

June nods yes. She's still trying to rock the attitude, like she doesn't need anyone's help.

'Great,' Quint says as he splits open the metal blinds, 'but that doesn't solve this problem.'

I walk over and peer through the blinds.

Big Mama is parked out front, where we left
her. She's surrounded by zombies. A hundred,
almost. OK, bad, but that's not the end of the
world. (No pun intended.) It's not like –

Ohhhh.

Farther out, across the street, I see something
colossally worse than zombies –

Blarg.

The monster is sitting on top of some poor
dude's house. The roof is caved in in the middle,
the wooden walls are bent at the sides, the
windows are shattered, and the front door is
popped open. Blarg is just perched there, waiting,
watching the school. The nerve of this Blarg . . .

I shut the blinds. 'So, June, little hiccup here. Nothing to lose our heads over. But it's not just zombies out there. It's also, um, Blarg.'

June crosses her arms. 'I'll probably regret asking this, but . . . what's a Blarg?'

'Blarg is a, uh, well – a big man-eating monster. With a bit of an attitude problem.'

'Mmm-hmm,' June says. 'And Jack, I'll probably regret asking this, too. But do you have any idea why this "Blarg" is here?' The annoyance in June's voice is about as thick as maple syrup.

I cough into my hand. 'Well, a few months back, I got into, just a, y'know, a little scuffle with him at the CVS. And I, well –'

'You what?' June growls.

I stabbed him in the forehead.

June looks like she's about to punch me in the nose. 'Well, you weren't kidding,' she says, peeking through the blinds. 'He is big.'

'And he's just chilling out!' I exclaim. 'He's watching the school and watching Big Mama. Waiting for us to make a move. Y'know, I've had enough of this guy . . .'

I yank up the blinds and throw open the window. 'Hey, Blarg! LEAVE ME ALONE! JUST GET OUTTA HERE, MONSTER JERK!'

'Jack, you fool!' Quint says, and runs to the window.

Blarg's ear holes open and his big head cranes from side to side. He hops down off the house. The windows rattle as he hits the ground, no more than two hundred feet from us. His head jerks around again. He's sniffing. Hunting for the source of my voice.

'Look at that thing!' Dirk says. 'He's so dumb, he can't even see us up here!'

I shake my head. 'He's not dumb. He's the opposite. Of all these monsters out there, he's the smartest. He's got, like, a vendetta against me.'

'That's why you don't stab monsters in the forehead, Jack,' June says.

'Look, lesson learned, OK? In the future, I'll try to minimize all monster forehead stabbings.'

Blarg is stomping closer when he almost trips over a car. The massive monster stumbles before catching himself.

Quint lets out a 'Hmmm . . .'

'What are you *hmmm*ing about?' June asks.

Quint runs over to a desk and whips out his dictionary-sized three-ring research binder. The rest of us crowd around, watching Quint flip through pages. Every few moments, he'll pause, think for a moment, then continue flipping.

Finally, he stops on one of my photographs and says, 'Jack, you magnificent son of a gun!'

'Why? What? I did something good? I mean, obviously I did – but uh, which good thing are you talking about?'

Quint spins the book around.

Quint's going a mile a minute now. 'Your photos, Jack. I told you they were useful! See this one here – the one you took when you first fought Blarg at CVS? See how Blarg's eyes are pale white and sort of see-through?'

'Yeah, so . . . ?'

'That means his low-light vision is poor! That's why he tripped over that car just now. He's built for hunting during the day!'

'Wait . . . so is he, like, waiting for the sun to come up?' I ask. 'Knowing that then we'll come out and he can finish me off, once and for all?'

Quint swallows. Nods. 'I think so.'

'So we need to go NOW!' I exclaim. 'Before it's light out! And it's almost dawn now!'

Quint sighs and runs his hand through his hair. 'And how do we even do that? There are hundreds of zombies out there. We need armour to get to Big Mama. We need weapons! Where are we going to find that stuff in a school!?'

Quint's right.

I lean against Mr Vogel's desk. My head hangs. We're trapped. Trapped like rats. Trapped like trapped rats in a giant rat trap made for trapping rats.

And the worst part of it is – this is 100% my fault. I never should have come to save June. She didn't need saving. She didn't need me at all. And now everyone's stuck here.

Suddenly –

Jack Sullivan, stop hanging your head. You came to rescue me. I'm giving you a shot. So figure it out.

I catch the tennis ball just before it conks me in the nose. I spin it around in my hand. And BAM! I got it!

OK, guys, find armour. Find weapons. Anything that'll help us make the walk to Big Mama.

Dirk grins. 'Oh yeah. I like this.'

Dirk and June and Quint split up, wandering through the huge gym storage closet, looking for anything that might be helpful.

But I have everything I need. Actually, everything I need except for . . .

Ball-player Eye Black! Sports war-paint, for looking like one bad dude! Like a tough-guy outfielder!

I grab a tin. *Now* I have everything I need.

I take a seat. I'm trying to clear my mind, hold down the fear, when Quint walks over, looking frustrated. 'I don't see anything for me.'

'Just find something to protect yourself with, buddy,' I say.

Quint frowns. 'I don't want to just protect myself, friend. I want to help fight! I want to really, well, sock it to those zombies!'

'Dude, you usually just want to hang back while Dirk and I go out and get our butts kicked. What gives now?'

Quint sort of blushes. Then he gestures with his head, across the room. I follow his nod – and I see June, digging through a box.

'What? June?' I say. 'You want to look brave in front of June? Hey, June's mine! I got dibs!'

'There's no dibs on girls, Jack!'

'And I don't think you know how girls work! She doesn't like you! If she likes anyone, it's me!'

'Jack, relax,' Quint says, holding his hands up all defensively. 'I know you like June. I'm not out to steal your girl. I just – well, she *is* a girl. And I'd prefer not to look lame in front of her.'

Ah. I nod. Understood.

Quint's eyes light up. 'I've got it! I shall return!' He dashes across the gym and out the door. I can only imagine what fantastic absurdity he's concocting.

About twenty minutes later, June and Dirk are finished arming themselves, when –

I'm back! Everybody can stop worrying now!

What the huh?! Quint's not wearing anything different! Just his same dorky lab coat.

'Quint! You're supposed to be getting armoured here!

'Oh, I am armoured,' he says. 'Armoured . . . WITH SCIENCE!'

All right then – Quint wins the award for dorkiest sentence ever spoken. Quint yanks open his lab coat and reveals . . .

Quint's Tactical Chemistry Belt!

Dirk frowns. 'How are you supposed to punch anything with that?'

I shrug. 'OK, Quint, you're right. That's pretty rad.'

'I've got something for you, too, friend,' Quint says, reaching into his back pocket. My eyes go wide as he reveals: my Wrist-Rocket.

'I took it from Mr Mando's desk,' he says. 'Remember he confiscated it from you? For shooting pennies at chemical flasks?'

I nod as I take the Wrist-Rocket and feel the weight of it in my hand. It's a serious slingshot.

Dirk is suddenly behind us, draping his arms over Quint and me and looking at June.

'Well, lady?' Dirk asks. 'How do we look?'

June scrunches up her eyes. 'Hmm . . .'

She grabs my hand, pulling me from Dirk's grip, and we all cross the gym. I won't lie – June's hand on mine is basically the greatest thing since sliced pizza.

There's a big mirror on one wall – the one we use for dance month.

I take in the image. I mean, sure, we look like a bunch of down-on-our-luck losers who have no business fighting monsters, hatching plans or really attempting *anything*.

But hey, we are . . .

A TEAM!

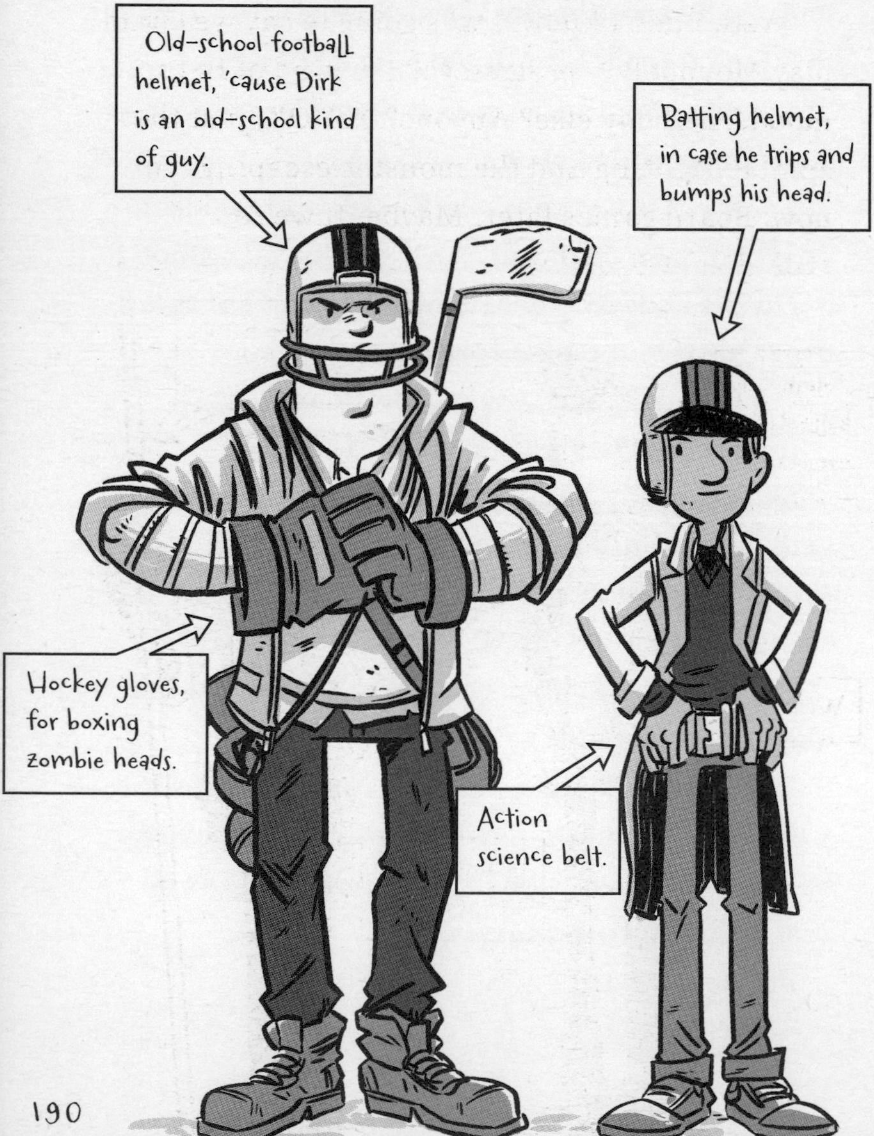
Old-school football helmet, 'cause Dirk is an old-school kind of guy.
Batting helmet, in case he trips and bumps his head.
Hockey gloves, for boxing zombie heads.
Action science belt.

'Now what?' Dirk says.

'Now we get to Big Mama,' I say. 'And get back to the tree house. And then . . .'

'There's more?' June asks.

'Well, I don't know. I was going to say we could play Monopoly? Or Stratego? I'm kind of in the mood. Anybody else? Anyone? No? OK, just the zombie-fighting and the monster-escaping. For now. Board games later. Maybe. If we're still alive. OK, let's go.'

chapter fifteen

At the end of the school's long side hallway is
a metal door. I hold my breath and push on
the safety handle.

It's nearly pitch black outside. My eyes
adjust, and in the moonlight, I see zombies.
Zombies everywhere. And Blarg, across the
street, staring vacantly into the night.

'OK, crew,' I whisper. 'Stay quiet. AND NO
LIGHT!'

'What light would there be?!' Dirk asks.

'I dunno – if you're carrying a lightsaber,
don't whip it out all of a sudden. Just no
light. OK?'

They all nod.

'I really wish we had a secret handshake
or something right now,' I say.

'Jack, give up on the secret handshake,'
Quint says. 'There are no secret handshakes.'

'There will be!' I say. 'Once we get home
alive. Now – ready?'

We all look at each other. Thinking about
what we're about to do. Nervous. Terrified,
right down to the bone. But in this together.

We all nod our heads yes, then I step out the door.

We move very stealthily.

Very stealthily, for about seven feet. Seven feet of super Prince-of-Persia-style stealthiness before the zombies catch scent of our human stink.

The undead monsters moan and roar and open their arms, waiting to greet us with their decaying fingers and sink their teeth into our skin and just straight-up peel the flesh from our bones!

Suddenly, all around me, it's freaking crazy zombie-battling action! Fists fly! Bones crunch!

Dirk is throwing haymakers. *POW!* One hard uppercut to a zombie chin.

June swings her broom-handle spear. *KRAK!* It slams against zombie skull. Then she whirls, swinging low, sweeping four undeaders off their feet.

SMASH! Quint cracks one of his glass tubes against an undead head. He's blinding them with science!

We continue forward, battling, fighting, forcing our way to Big Mama. We're getting close, just one final push!

Good job, guys! Good effort!

Dirk yanks open the door to Big Mama, and then the worst possible thing that could happen – well, it happens.

Big Mama's headlights snap on. The high beams. They cut across the grass, slicing through the darkness. I follow their path. They're shining directly onto Blarg. His eyes flash and he opens his fanged mouth and he lets out a tremendous 'BLARGGGGG!!!!!!'

'Jack!' Quint shrieks. 'You left the high beams on?!?!?!' He turns them off fast.

'Whoops. Look, I said I was a good driver. I never said I was a good dashboard-controller guy.'

'BLARGGGGG!!!!!!'

Blarg takes a dozen heavy, Earth-quaking steps, and in moments he's towering over Big Mama. His next step shakes the ground and sends us all tumbling back onto our butts.

I'm sprawled out, staring up at the fiend.

And that's when I see it. Right in front of my eyes: my sneakers.

And it hits me! A backup plan!

Heroes GOTTA have backup plans!

I reach down and – *RIP!* – yank off the tape covering my Light-Upz. The red lights glow bright in the darkness as I get to my feet.

'Jack, what are you doing?!' June hisses.

'Dancing!'

'WHAT?!'

Fun fact: I am a fantastically bad dancer. All my own moves – a little bit of the robot dance, a little bit of a jig, a little bit shaking and convulsing, and a little bit Cotton-Eyed Joe.

Blarg's eyes flicker as he focuses on the flashing lights. He groans curiously.

And then . . .

'See you later, guys!' I call, and I take off running.

'Where are you going?!' June shouts.

'Just running! You get to the tree house!'

'Wait, Jack, take this!' Quint calls after me.

I turn, stumbling, just in time to see Quint tossing one of his little science-dork action capsules toward me. A terrible throw, as always. I scoop it up and keep running. 'What is it?' I call out.

'Acid Eye Blast!' Quint shouts.

'Neat name! Now get out of here!' I yell, spinning around and racing across the grass, out into the street. Bright-red lights flashing with every step. Blarg roars and stomps after me.

This is the dumbest thing I've ever done. By far. And I've done A LOT of dumb things. I mean, I'm the guy who once licked Old Spice deodorant because I thought it was classier than teeth-brushing.

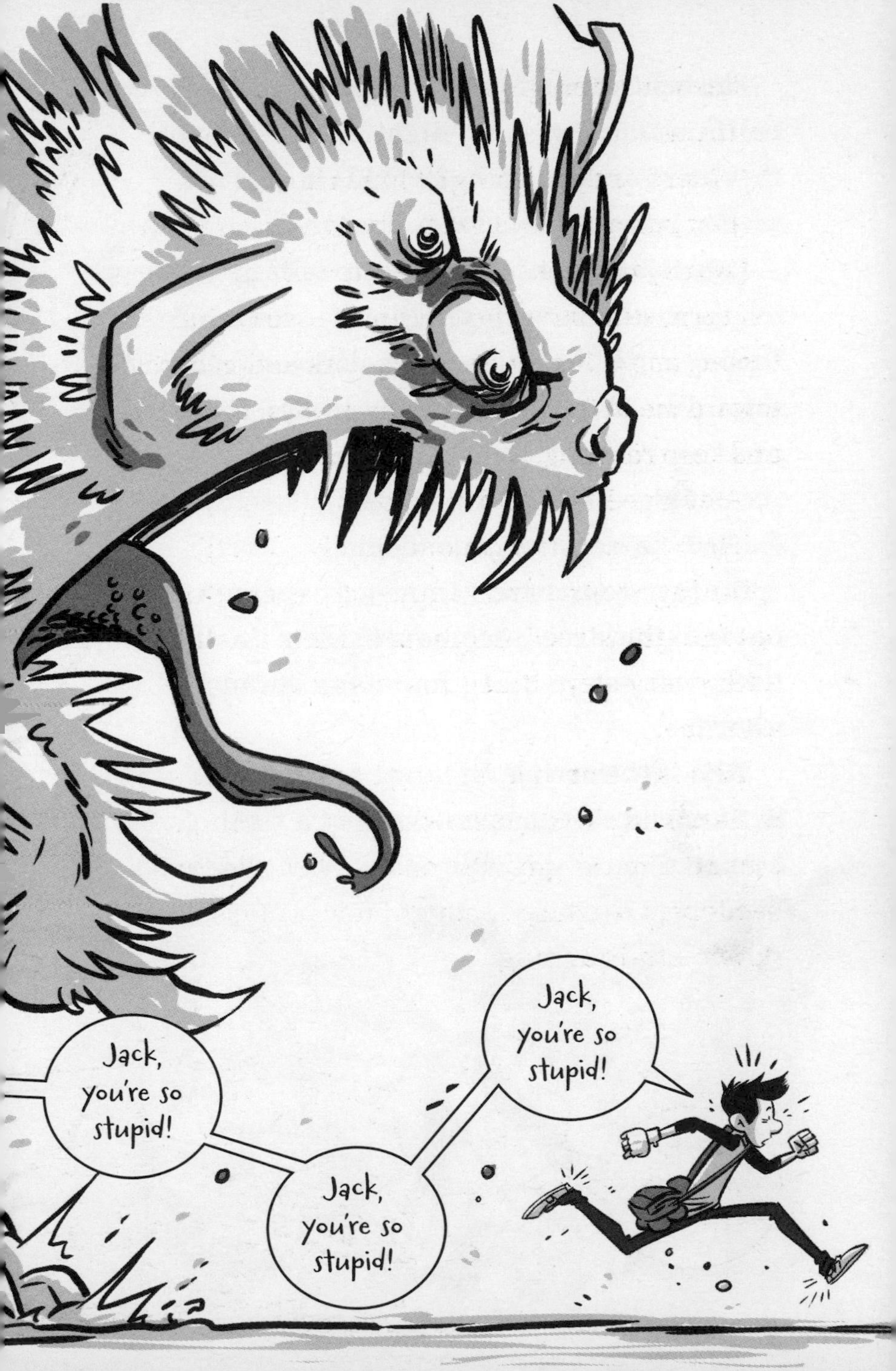
Jack, you're so stupid!
Jack, you're so stupid!
Jack, you're so stupid!

Far behind me, I hear Big Mama's engine roar to life, rumbling in the night. Well, I suppose that's a silver lining. Even if Blarg eats me whole, I gave my friends a chance.

I continue running, continue racing, continue telling myself how stupid this is – down Spring Street, across Main Street, and up onto the sidewalk. And there, dead ahead of me, is a big overturned truck. I slide to a halt. To my left is the pet store. Cars all along the sidewalk. I've dashed directly into a dead end.

Blarg tramps closer. Immense. Gigantic. Looming over me is a creature from another time, another place – a horrible nightmare figure.

Well, Mr Horrible Nightmare Figure, ol' Jack Sullivan doesn't go down without a fight . . . And he doesn't go down without his Wrist-Rocket.

Let's dance, monster pants!

Blarg takes a heavy step toward me, shaking the pavement, nearly knocking me off my feet. His hot breath blasts my face as he opens his thick, toothy mouth, and unleashes an ear-splitting RAWWWWWRRR!!!

Lightning fast, my hands flash to the acid capsule in my pocket, yank it out, jam it into the slingshot, tug it back, wait. I hold my breath like Robin Hood lining up an arrow, and FLING!

A demonic howl erupts from Blarg's lungs. He paws at his face, trying to wipe away the sizzling chemical mixture. YEE-HAW! I've damaged the blasted beast! Acid Eye Blast for the win!

'What's up now, Blarg?!' I shout.

Blarg lowers his hand then, and reveals . . . Well, I just about puke all over my Light-Upz.

Quint's acid capsule has done something to the monster. He's changed. He is now . . .

Acid Blarg!

Acid bubbling on forehead wound.

Smells worse than he did last time around, somehow.

So this is it. The monster has taken his FINAL FORM!

THUD!

Noise behind me. And then a fuming, ferocious growl. ANOTHER monster? C'mon! Can't a fella get a break?! Just, like, two seconds without a new monster assault would be HEAVEN!

I spin around to see –

Chemically mangled mug.

Look on his face like, 'THIS TIME IT'S PERSONAL!'

chapter sixteen

Rover!!!

Rover slams into me from behind, taking me off my legs, knocking me up into the air. I grab the reins and work my way up his furry side.

'Rover, buddy!' I shout. 'Nice timing!'

I duck as Rover charges between Acid Blarg's legs. And then –

WE'RE OFF!

I grip the reins as tight as an Xbox controller while Rover rockets down the street, massive paws pounding pavement. He rips around the corner and I'm nearly launched from the saddle.

KA-KRASH!

Rover lowers his head and slams into a trash can, knocking it up and over my head. An old burger wrapper plasters itself to my face. Yuck. Pickles. Old pickle juice on my tongue. I rip off the gnarly pickle wrapper in time to see –

Dozers in the road!

'ROVER, GIVE IT TO 'EM!' I scream, ducking down, and –

KA-POW!

Acid Blarg snarls as he chases us. He's moving faster now – practically on top of us. I can smell his foul stench. But we're close! The tree house is just two blocks away . . . The sun is coming up.

'Faster, Rover!'

And then I spot Big Mama, racing down the street. I see Dirk's behind the wheel. I tug the reins, steering Rover until we're sprinting alongside the speeding truck.

'Hey, buddies!' I call out. 'How fun is this?!'

Dirk glances out the window and does a double-take. June sits up, catches my eye and smiles. I flash a wink, like a cool guy.

I catch a glimpse of Quint reaching into his pocket, grabbing his little remote control keychain thing. It's all like, *BEEP-BOOP-BOOP!*

The tree house towers over the fence at the end of the street. It's going into action, almost transforming, as all of Quint's gadgets and defences begin activating.

The tree house's catapult flings forward, launching a big-screen TV. It soars through the air, tumbling, end over end. I crane my neck in time to see –

Dirk steers Big Mama up onto the kerb and the truck skids to a halt. My friends move in a unit, like a better-looking version of the Avengers, racing to the fence and climbing over.

A second later, Rover charges forward, smashing through the fence, into the backyard. In a flash, I'm climbing off Rover, scaling the tree house, ready for the final battle at dawn . . .

chapter seventeen

Quint rushes around the tree house in a panic. Below us, I spot Dirk running for Quint's garage workshop. Entire trees are knocked down, ripped from the earth, as Acid Blarg stomps closer. His thick black claws swing like great blades.

June's face is so white, it's nearly see-through. 'Let's keep running!' she shrieks. 'We can't stay! He's going to rip this tree house from the ground.'

But we can't do that. I can't do that.

Because see, here's the thing. Here's the truth. This tree house isn't just any old tree house. It's my home. For the first time in my life I have a real, permanent home.

And Quint and June and Dirk – for the first time in my life, I have real friends. Permanent ones. Not-going-anywhere ones. A family.

Everything I was ever jealous of – everything those other kids had, when I felt like a crummy orphan. Well, now I have it.

Sure, it took the freaking MONSTER APOCALYPSE for me to get it. But there's no way I'm losing it now.

Not to this big jerk.

I grip the tree house railing. Acid Blarg's next step crushes the fence around the backyard. Another crushes our wooden pike things.

'Outer defences breached!' Quint hollers.

So, a fact about Little Hug juice barrels – they're the best. If you've never had 'em, get 'em. They're sweet and delicious and taste like sugary chemicals – and when they're empty, they make for perfect monster-stopping juice grenades.

Quint concocted a killer recipe.

Little Hug Monster-Stopping Juice Grenades!

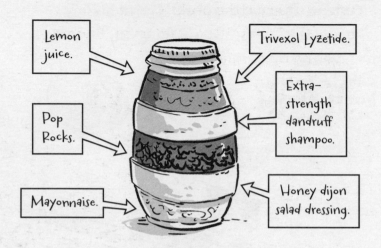

Lemon juice.

Trivexol Lyzetide.

Extra-strength dandruff shampoo.

Pop Rocks.

Mayonnaise.

Honey dijon salad dressing.

Acid Blarg howls as the liquid grenade concoctions crackle against his hardened head. He claws at his sizzling skin.

'JACK, THE SECOND CATAPULT!' Quint yells.

'You, um – you guys have a second catapult?' June asks.

'Duh!' I say with a grin, then leap to a dangling rope and swing around to the other side of the tree house. There, Quint has a giant branch pulled back and tied to the floor of the tree house deck. The second catapult.

The catapult basket is a rusty old refrigerator box, stocked with crud from around town: bike seats, microwaves, bricks, car doors.

Time to unleash the junk!

I bring the Louisville Slicer down, hacking through the rope, and –

JUNK ATTACK!

A whole double ton of junk nails Acid Blarg on the nose. A bucket of bowling balls slams into his belly and the hideous beast howls.

But still, this unstoppable evil keeps coming. Marching forward like some murderous monster machine . . .

'I'll distract him!' June shouts. She leaps, swinging on the escape rope, out and over the yard to the roof of my neighbours' house. I grin. June's a natural.

Acid Blarg turns his big head to June. That gives Rover the opening he needs to jump in, diving at Acid Blarg's feet, digging his thick fangs into the monster's leg. Acid Blarg roars and reaches down, scooping up Rover and hurling him –

Quint and Rover tumble over the side of the tree house. Rover yelps as he hits the ground. Quint lands, hard, on the grass. I hear him go *OOF* as the wind is taken out of him.

I'm spun aside.

The Louisville Slicer slips from my hand and sticks into the grass, just inches from Quint's face.

We can't keep this up much longer.

But then –

The cavalry has arrived!

Pick on someone your own size!

Dirk is armed to the teeth with Quint's insane inventions! He flings four razor Frisbees through the air, then unloads with the explosive football launcher.

BLAM! BLAM! BLAM!

The hits muddle Acid Blarg's monster brain. He takes an off-balance step forward, into the moat pool, and –

KA-SPLASH!

There's an ear-splitting *KRAK* as Acid Blarg's giant, tree-trunk-sized ankle snaps. The monster is wounded!

This is the moment . . . Post-Apocalyptic Action Hero Jack Sullivan's moment!

'Quint,' I call down. 'Let's play catch!'

Quint, on the grass, looks up at me – confused. And then – *ding!* – he gets it. 'But you can't catch! And I can't throw!' he shouts.

'Today we can! Today we WILL!'

Quint nods once, hard. He scrambles to his feet, reaches out and grabs the Louisville Slicer.

His face is pale. Sweat pouring down his forehead. We have one shot at this.

I charge across the tree house, take two steps on the diving board, and shout, 'NOW!'

Quint throws the Louisville Slicer.

I jump up, hanging in mid-air for a moment –

The bat spins up, up, up as I'm hitting the board, and then I'm springing into the air, and –

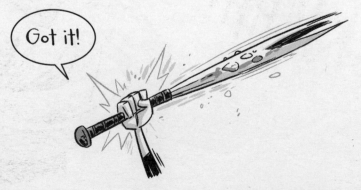

Got it!

218

I grip the handle tight as I'm twisting, my
body turning in the air as I pull back the blade,
and –

SKICHH!

I slam the Louisville Slicer into the scar on
Acid Blarg's giant monster forehead. He howls.
I'm dangling from the blade, gripping tight,
as the monster's legs give out and he comes
crashing down down down, and –

BOOM!!

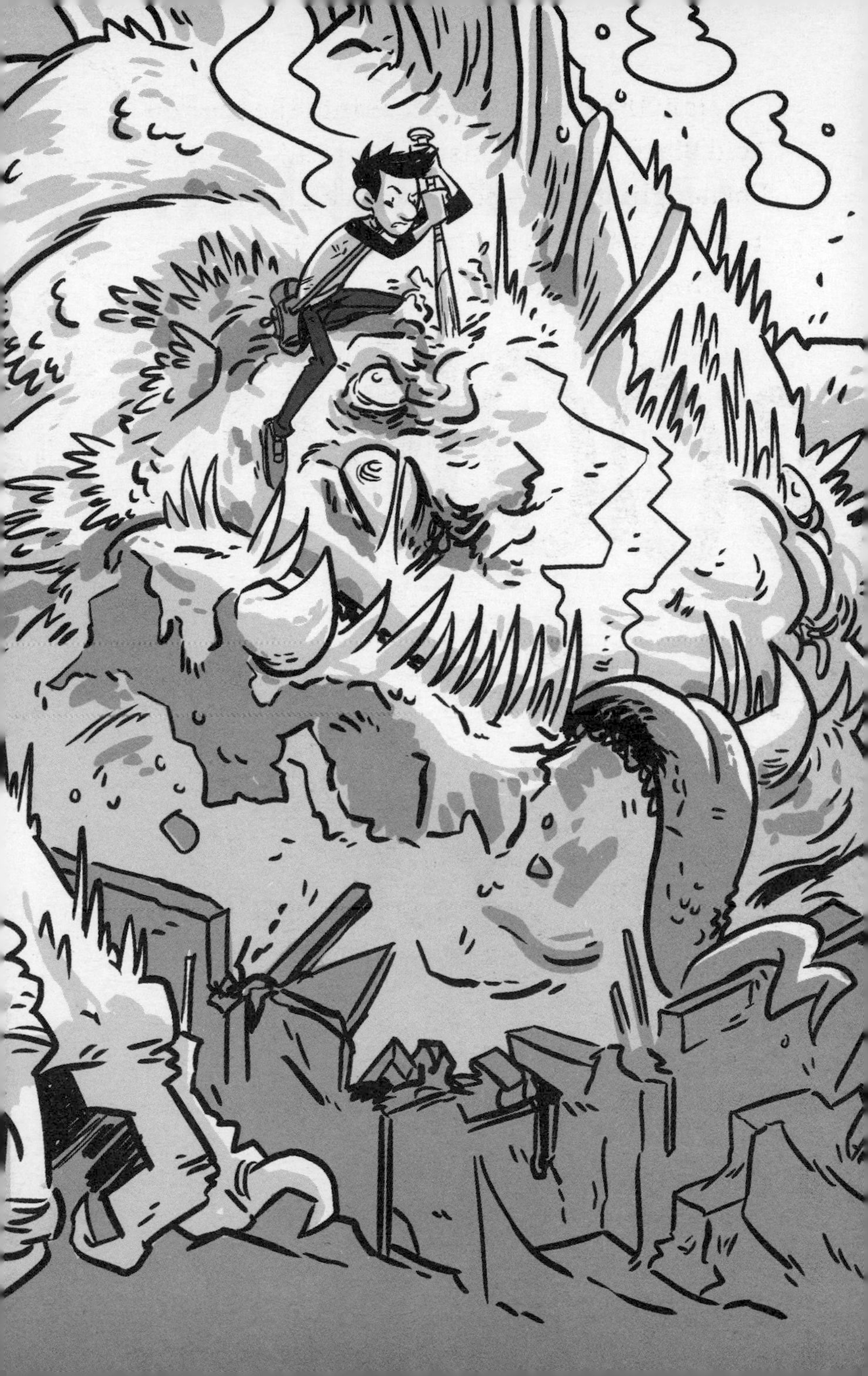

chapter eighteen

I lie there, on top of big dead Blarg, trying to catch my breath. It takes about, oh, two hours.

I don't hear any of the terrible sounds of this world. No monsters howling, no zombies moaning.

Just my breath, returning to me.

And then – *OOMPH!*

A kick to my gut. My eyes flicker open.

Hey, jerk.

Nice job.

I manage a grin. 'I know.'

Silence, for a moment. Then I hear Quint and Dirk rustling around. Rover yawns.

June has her hands on her hips, taking it all in: the ragged ground, the giant dead monster we're standing on, the kick-butt tree fort that towers over the yard – and Dirk and Quint and Rover, our friends. And then she smiles and says, 'Well, that was something.'

'Yep,' I say. 'It sure was.'

'Hey, dork! Stop smiling!' Dirk hollers, grinning.

'Yes,' Quint says. 'We've got much cleaning up to do. And a tree house to re-arm.'

A tree house to re-arm. A home to defend. And you know what? It feels great.

So that's it.

We won.

We survived. For now . . .

There are more monsters to fight and more beasts to slay. And hopefully there are more kids out there, and the tree house's numbers will grow.

Someday, maybe, we'll lead an army against these monsters.

But until then, the most important thing is . . . I did it!

Well, sorta . . . I mean, it turns out June was no damsel in distress. And she most definitely did *not* need rescuing. But, in a roundabout way, I rescued her anyway!

And that means –

I completed the ULTIMATE Feat of Apocalyptic Success!

And now?

Well, now, I think it's time we all relaxed. At least for a little while. And hey – maybe we'll even have time to figure out a secret team handshake before the next giant monster comes around the corner . . .

THE END!
(for now . . .)

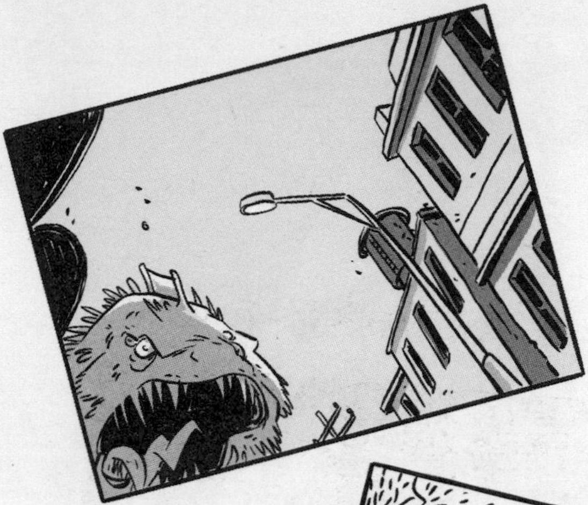
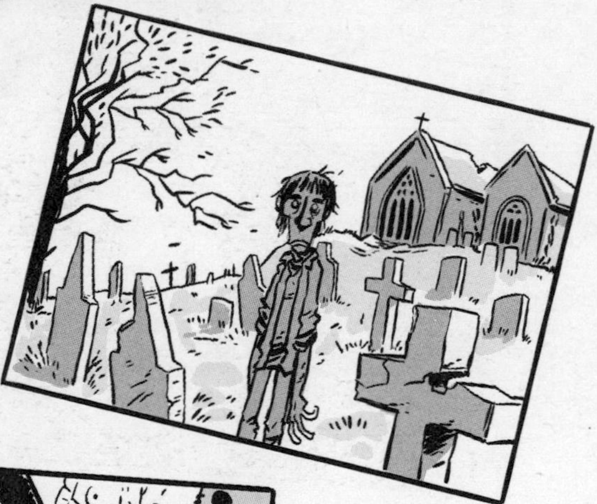
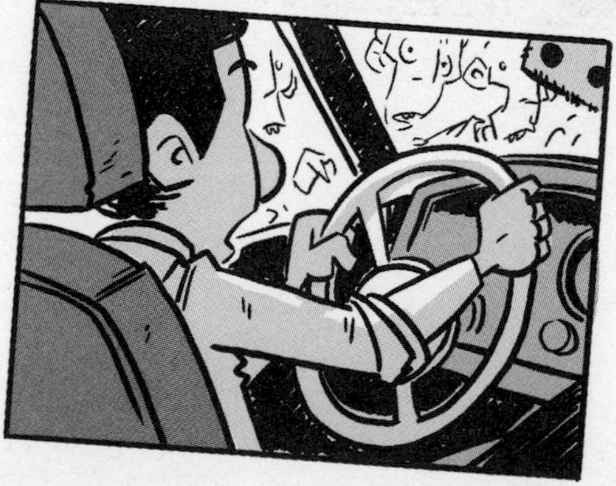

Snapshots from Jack's camera!

Acknowledgments

Doug Holgate – who brought this faint notion of mine to life in ways beyond my wildest dreams – there aren't enough superlatives for your talent. My brilliant editor, Leila Sales, for redefining the word *patience* – so smart, so perceptive, such a brilliant grasp of story. Jim Hoover for just 'getting' this thing from day one and working his butt off to make it amazing. Ken Wright, for believing this could work.

For Bridget Hartzler, publicist rated grade-A awesome. Jeff Kinney, for his encouragement and generosity. And it should go without saying, my tough-nosed agent Dan Lazar, for two a.m. e-mail responses and trying so hard to make this thing happen. Torie Doherty-Munro, for answering dumb question after dumb question. And for suggestions and thoughts and ideas (good and bad), much thanks to Mike Mandolese, Wes Ryan, Geoff Baker, all the members of the N.S.S., and – as always – Ben Murphy.

And above all, thank you, Mom – thank you for never calling me in before dinner; thank you for always allowing me to find my own adventures in the backyard; thank you for letting me scrape my knees and break some bones and have a tree house all my own; thank you for being the best mom ever. Now please, please, kids – stop reading all this boring acknowledgments crud and go get into some monster-sized adventures of your own.

MAX BRALLIER!

(maxbrallier.com) is the author of more than twenty books and games. He writes children's books and adult books, including the pick-your-own-path adventure *Can YOU Survive the Zombie Apocalypse*? He is the creator and writer of *Galactic Hot Dogs*, an ongoing middle-grade web serial, which was released as a book by Simon & Schuster in 2015. He writes for licensed properties including *Adventure Time*, *Regular Show*, *Steven Universe*, and *Uncle Grandpa*.

Under the pen name Jack Chabert, he is the creator and author of the Eerie Elementary series for Scholastic Books. He is a game designer for the crazy fun virtual world Poptropica and does freelance game design for numerous online properties. In the olden days, he worked in the marketing department at St. Martin's Press. Max lives in New York City with his wife, Alyse, who is way too good for him.

Follow Max on Twitter @MaxBrallier.

The author building his own tree house as a kiddo. This puppy was NOT seriously armed to the teeth.

DOUGLAS HOLGATE!

(www.skullduggery.com.au) has been a freelance
comic book artist and illustrator based in Melbourne,
Australia, for more than ten years. He's illustrated
books for publishers such as HarperCollins, Penguin
Random House, Hachette, and Simon & Schuster,
including the Planet Tad series, *Cheesie Mack*, *Case
File 13*, and *Zoo Sleepover*.

Douglas has illustrated comics for Image,
Dynamite, Abrams, and Penguin Random House.
He's currently working on the self-published series
Maralinga, which received grant funding from the
Australian Society of Authors and the Victorian
Council for the Arts, as well as the all-ages graphic
novel *Clem Hetherington and the Ironwood Race*,
published by Scholastic Graphix, both co-created
with writer Jen Breach.

Follow Douglas on Twitter @douglasbot.

Overnight, Jack Sullivan's life has become like the plot of a video game. So far, he's survived the **ZOMBIE APOCALYPSE** by hiding out in his treehouse. But now he has come up with his own...

ULTIMATE FEATS OF APOCALYPTIC SUCCESS:
1. Locate Quint Baker, best friend and inventor
2. Find and rescue June Del Toro, his secret love interest
3. Defeat Blarg, the biggest, baddest monster in town
4. Become a **ZOMBIE-FIGHTING, MONSTER-BASHING TORNADO OF COOL!**